LOVERS ON THE FRINGE

STEPHANIE JULIAN

SIZE MATTERS

Carrie Benton's got the best job in the world working as a reporter for the Weekly News Journal. Chupacabra picnicking at the Jersey Shore? Check. Aliens in the White House? Absolutely. Bigfoot stalking the forests of northern Pennsylvania? Well, okay…but Bigfoot is so Left Coast.

Tim Sattazahn can't believe his luck. The six-foot redhead who crashed into his forest during a snowstorm is gorgeous, funny and hot for him. Everything would be perfect…except that she's looking for Bigfoot.

And, unfortunately for Tim, she found him…

THE BIGGER THEY ARE…

Andy Lohani is in a serious funk. The Yeti shifter is looking for love, or at least some loving, and when he meets Jenna Durham one dark night, sparks fly. She's beautiful, sexy and hot for him. Getting her in his bed is job one. Unfortunately, she's Normal and he's really…not.

Accountant Jenna Durham doesn't believe her brother's crazy theories about Bigfoot and the Loch Ness Monster. But she agrees to check out a bar in northern Pennsylvania where her brother says Bigfoot hangs out. At least she's getting an expenses-paid weekend away.

When Jenna meets seven-foot blond and blue-eyed hunk Andy, she realizes she owes her brother one hell of an apology. Because she has a huge crush on the Abominable Snowman. But if she wants to keep him, she might have to give up her Normal life for one on the Fringe…

SIZE MATTERS

STEPHANIE JULIAN

Chapter One

"God damn freaking foreign cars."

Carrie Benton wrestled open the door of her Suzuki Sidekick piece of shit, swung her legs out then stepped into three feet of snow.

And promptly fell flat on her face when a wave of dizziness overtook her. Whoa. She must have smacked her head against the windshield harder than she'd thought when she'd plowed into that tree.

"God damn freaking snow."

Scrambling to her feet, she brushed white powder from her jeans and her favorite bright-green Liz Claiborne blazer, holding one hand to her head. Gonna have a lump there. At least there was no blood.

"I'm going to kill him. That son-of-a-no-good-god-damn-bastard."

Stalking to the front of the car, she stared at the crumpled bumper wrapped around the thick tree trunk on the side of the road. Steam seeped from beneath the hood.

"Great. Just freaking great."

She swung her foot at the useless bumper, knowing it was a stupid-ass thing to do. Luckily she was wearing her biker boots, the ones she'd picked up at an outlet for forty-five bucks a couple of years ago. They were her go-to shoes for mucking around in fields, woods, snow, rain and dark of night.

So, she wore them pretty much every day.

Especially today when it was below freezing, snowing like a bitch and she was out in the middle of *freaking* nowhere.

Alone.

With a busted car.

And a headache.

"And is that a smart-assed comment on my life, or what?" she said to no one in particular.

Of course, if Luke hadn't caught the stupid stomach virus that'd been going through the editorial office like rotten Mu Shu Pork through a dog, she wouldn't be alone.

She'd told him not to get too close to that intern with the big blue eyes and even bigger tits.

But no, he'd had to go sniffing around like a hound in heat. Just before he'd done his impression of Linda Blair in *The Exorcist*.

He hadn't even gotten laid for his trouble but he'd spent the last two days in bed, turning a shade of green reserved for moldy food.

Unfortunately, his head hadn't spun around completely. At least they could've used that as art for the *Weekly News Journal*.

"Photojournalist Possessed by the Devil" would've looked great on the front cover.

But now she was stuck, by herself, in a freaking snowstorm somewhere in the state game lands shared by Berks and Schuylkill Counties in southeastern Pennsylvania, all because her editor wanted a few photos for inside art.

"Hell, Care," Bill Dailey had bellowed. She didn't think the forty-something-ish, old-school journalist knew how to talk in a normal tone of voice. "We're only thirty minutes from ground zero. Go get some live shots to use for the page next week before the damn *Investigative Weekly* gets their asses in gear and beats us to the story in our own backyard. And if you actually see Bigfoot, make sure the zipper don't show."

Carrie had seen some weird shit in her five years as a reporter ("Reporter my ass," her father's voice taunted in her head) for the *Journal*.

Most could be explained.

Alien crop circles?

Kids with sticks and a few too many six packs of beer beating circles in a corn field.

Dinosaur rampaging through eastern Lebanon County?

An escaped bull tearing through neighbors' gardens in the middle of the night.

Sure, she'd come across one or two things she couldn't explain.

Cold spots, disembodied voices, Lady Gaga.

Unfortunately, Bigfoot was not one of them.

And now she had a broken car and a cell phone that wasn't picking up a signal.

She thought about swearing again but decided she'd rather do it in the car where it was still warm. But wouldn't be for long because she was down to less than a quarter of a tank of gas.

Yeah, yeah, she should have filled up before she'd left. Hell, she should've turned around when the snow began to fall fast and heavy a few minutes after she'd departed the newsroom in West Reading.

But no, here she was, miles from nowhere with not much gas, no food and a few thousand dollars in camera equipment.

Think, Carrie. You're not a stupid woman.

Well, not usually. This didn't qualify as one of her better days.

Staring down the snow-covered lane that looked like the setting for some sappy Christmas card, all she saw were brown tree trunks and white snow.

Okay, no one built a road to nowhere. She refused to believe people would be that stupid.

Of course, some of her readers really did believe in Bigfoot and Dracula, so...

No. There had to be a home somewhere along this road.

Grabbing her purse and her pink parka off the front seat, and ignoring the slight dizziness she attributed to fear of the unknown, she made sure the camera equipment was hidden on the floor behind the front seat before she locked the car.

Then she started walking.

* * * * *

Tim Sattazahn watched the red-haired goddess trudge through the snow as she kept up a running conversation with herself.

She obviously had a lot to talk about because she never shut up.

Tim didn't mind. It was nice to hear someone else's voice, even if every other word was a half-assed obscenity.

Besides, her dirty mouth was turning him on.

She'd used "freaking" more times in one sentence than he'd ever heard other women say in their lives. Most of them she used in reference to someone named Bill.

He hoped Bill had his health insurance paid up because this woman was going to kick his ass when she got home. And from the looks of her, Tim figured she could do it.

Her legs looked long, lean and athletic in a pair of skintight jeans. The rest of her was bundled into a blindingly pink parka but he couldn't imagine the rest of the body wouldn't fit the legs.

Damn, the woman was gorgeous. He just hoped she wasn't

seriously injured.

He'd been out gathering wood when he'd heard the car engine chugging along. He'd had just enough time to wonder what the hell someone was doing out here in the middle of what was expected to be a two-day storm when he'd heard the unmistakable crunch of metal-on-tree-trunk.

As the only resident within a forty-mile radius, he'd known he had to check it out. The driver or passengers could be injured. They might need help.

He hadn't been close enough to alert her to his presence when he saw her leave the car and start walking, which he wouldn't have done anyway. He'd started to make his way toward her, keeping out of sight, but even he'd been bogged down in the fast-falling snow.

As he'd gotten closer, he'd slowed, not wanting to scare the crap out of her by barreling up to her, especially not the way he looked now. But he would try to herd her in the right direction if she wandered off the track, now nearly invisible in the snow.

In the five or so years since he'd lived here, only three people had ever found the dirt track leading to his home. Just dumb luck that she'd found it in the snow.

If she kept walking, she'd reach his house in a few minutes. It sent a shiver up his spine that had nothing to do with the cold. It'd been a while since he'd had anyone in his home, much less someone who looked like a Valkyrie.

She had to be nearly six feet tall, with autumn-red hair in a braid down her back and a body that made his blood run hot. All long limbs, lush curves, full mouth and big eyes. She could have stepped straight out of a Titian masterpiece. Aphrodite or Danae.

He wanted her. No two ways about it.

But she had to be injured. No one in their right mind would leave their car in the middle of a snowstorm to wander off.

At least she wore that parka that stood out against the snow like a neon sign.

One that winked out of sight as he passed behind a tree.

Oh shit.

He took off at a gallop, not caring if he scared her. Plowing through the almost-knee-high blanket of white, he covered the distance in a matter of seconds.

She lay sprawled on the snow, her coat and jeans an odd stain on all that white, her hair like one long stream of blood.

He lifted her into his arms, his gaze going to her full red lips. They were parted slightly as she breathed. Good. But her skin was ashen and chilled and she must have passed out because she didn't open her eyes and start to scream when she got a load of him.

Careful not to hurt her, he gathered her against his chest and headed home.

* * * * *

Carrie woke to pitch black.

She was naked and warm, cocooned between firm, hot silk and soft, warm cotton.

No, not silk. Skin.

Okay, that was interesting. Not bad, just... She didn't remember going home from the bar with a guy last night.

In fact, she couldn't remember going to Third and Spruce last night.

And this didn't feel like home.

What she did feel was safe. And Carrie always trusted her instincts. Before she'd taken the job with the *Journal,* her father had praised her ability to assess any situation in seconds.

Right now, she sensed the absolute security of her surroundings and the desire emanating from the man—definitely a man—holding her on his lap.

What she couldn't remember was how she'd gotten here.

She wriggled a little closer to the guy, felt his arms tighten around her and the hard ridge of his erection press against the bare skin of her thigh.

Wow, the guy was huge! Long and thick and... Oh, baby, she really *had* gotten lucky last night.

Turning her head, she reached out with one hand and encountered firm muscle. His arm flexed under her touch as she smoothed her way up to his broad shoulder then trailed her fingertips over his chest.

And rubbed her thigh against that enticing organ.

Thank God she'd shaved her legs yesterday.

The guy groaned into her hair. "Carrie..."

Oh, good. He remembered her name. Too bad she was drawing a blank on his.

Didn't matter. Obviously, she'd gone home with him last night. Maybe she was still a little drunk, not just hung over.

But that ache between her legs… Damn it, she wanted sex. Now.

The dark closed so tightly around them, she could barely see his outline but she moved both hands up and up his body until she finally reached his face. Wow, he must be really tall and she meant *really* tall because she was no slouch.

At five-ten—without heels which she wore anyway because she looked damn good in them—she typically had a few inches on most men. And of course, she was the kind of girl who liked her men big and strong.

Which made sense of why she'd gone home with this one.

Stubble roughened his broad jaw, sending a shiver of lust through her and causing her to rub against his cock again. God, she loved to hear men groan. It made her feel all powerful, like Wonder Woman. Or that FBI chick from *Fringe*. She loved that show. Hell, she'd marry JJ Abrams in a heartbeat. The guy had a better imagination than most of the yahoos she worked with.

And she worked with some of the best in the field. Granted, the field wasn't huge but…

With one hand, she traced his lips, pushing the other into his hair. The guy had lots of it. Down to his shoulders, at least.

Another point in his favor. She must've thought she'd hit the lottery last night. Wherever that had been.

And who cared about that now? Shifting around was a little difficult in the dark and she didn't want to hurt anything vital—namely that gorgeous erection—but with a little help from him, she wound up with her knees on either side of his thighs as he sat upright, her hands on his cheeks and her mouth descending on his.

He seemed surprised at first, his body freezing into stillness, but when she licked at his lips, he got with the program and kissed her back. And great freaking Jesus, the guy could kiss.

His tongue dove into her mouth and twined around hers while his hands grabbed onto her hips and pulled her even closer.

God, he was *huge*. And she didn't just mean his cock. Pressed against him the way she was now, she got a better sense of his size.

Her breasts were cushioned against a chest so broad and muscular, the guy had to be built like John Cena, the professional wrestler one of the girls at the *Journal* had a crush on.

His abs felt like a washboard, which she discovered when she pressed forward to rub her mound against his cock, looking for some relief for the tension in her body.

He broke away from her kiss, but his hips rose slightly, rubbing his cock almost where she needed it to go. Just a little to the left and he'd rub against her clit.

"Whoa, Carrie." His hands tightened on her hips but didn't push her away. "Are you sure you're feeling okay?"

Hmm, maybe she'd had more to drink last night than she remembered. But he was so nice to ask.

"I feel fine." She trailed one hand down his chest, fingers brushing against the tip of his cock. "And you feel amazing."

She wished she knew his name but didn't want to embarrass herself or him by asking for it. Later, after she satisfied this urge to jump his bones, she'd figure it out.

Right now...not caring so much.

Especially when she wrapped one hand around his cock and realized her fingers didn't meet.

Thank you, Goddess of...well, whatever goddess handled huge guys with accessories to match.

Warm flesh pulsed in her hand as she stroked from fat root to bulbous tip. Silky soft skin slid over the hard core and a drop of moisture seeped from the slit.

Using her thumb, she smeared the liquid over the head as she felt one of his hands leave her hip to trail over her ribs to cup her breast as he groaned deep in his chest. Long fingers kneaded her, pinching the nipple into a hard, aching point.

Nuzzling her nose in his neck, she breathed in deep, his scent musky woodsy and a little smoky. Kind of like sex and good barbecue.

Did he taste as good as he smelled? She flicked his skin with her tongue. Salty, heady. All man.

Yumm-O, as Rachael Ray would say about some thirty-minute, fat bomb of a meal. If this was the main course, who needed freakin' dessert?

She went back for seconds, licking from his neck to his earlobe, nipping the little piece of flesh and hearing his breath catch in his throat.

The hand on her breast tightened and, finally, he released the leash he'd been keeping on himself.

With another groan, he lifted his other hand from her hip to cup her unattended breast. She arched to give him better access and the motion rubbed her sex against his cock again. She clenched around nothing, needing something to fill her and fast. But with his fingers on her breasts, she was left with only one choice.

"Condom," she said. "Right now."

Tim heard Carrie say the magic word.

She wanted him to get a condom. Great freakin' Jesus, he was gonna get laid.

If he didn't come in her hand first, which was a very real possibility if she kept pumping him with her fist and rubbing herself against him.

And since he wasn't about to look a gift horse in the mouth, he released her breasts, wrapped his arms around her and stood to carry her to his bed in the loft.

It was pitch black in the house but he didn't need lights to get around. He had the layout memorized, even if it was his little head doing the thinking.

With Carrie a soft mass of sweet-smelling flesh in his arms, he took the stairs two at a time. With perfect aim, he tossed her on the bed, heard her gasp then start to laugh. Damn, she had a great laugh. Husky, low and just a little dirty.

His cock throbbed with each beat of his heart as he studied every curve, every line. He'd looked his fill earlier, downstairs, but that had been to make sure she didn't have any overt injuries.

Once he'd realized she'd just fainted, he'd stripped them both to warm her better in front of the fire and wrapped blankets around them as they sat on the couch. He'd figured he get her in one of his t-shirts and in bed before she woke.

But she'd felt damn good on his lap, so he'd held onto her.

He'd be a liar if he said he didn't want to screw her brains out. Hell, he'd take thank-you-for-saving-me sex over no sex at all.

Propping herself on her elbows, she tilted her head to the side, as if studying him, though he knew she wouldn't be able to see him as clearly as he could see her. His ancestors had developed incredible eyesight over the centuries. All that cave and forest dwelling.

Still, she had to realize he was taller than anyone she'd probably ever met before.

"You really are a big guy, aren't you?" she murmured.

He stilled. "I won't hurt you, Carrie."

"Oh, I don't think it'll hurt," she said, rising to her knees on the bed and reaching unerringly for his waist. "But I'm dying to get you inside me."

Her words made his balls tighten in response, his cock twitching with anticipation, and he was about to reach for the bedside table and the condoms he kept there when she wound her arms around his back, pulled him close and sealed her mouth on his chest.

He sucked in a deep breath and held it as she placed slow, drugging kisses from the center of his chest to his right nipple, where she opened her mouth to tongue it into a stiff point. Then she moved to the left nipple and did the same there.

With a groan, his hands fell on her shoulders, pulling her body even closer against his. With her gorgeous breasts almost exactly where he wanted them, he thrust his hips slightly, brushing his cock against her sternum.

She got the hint and moved her hands from his hips to her breasts, pushing the mounds together until they encased his cock in soft flesh.

Aw, hell. Now this was heaven. His eyelids dropped shut for a few brief seconds while he let himself soak in the gut-tightening sensation of his cock rubbing between her breasts.

So fucking good. Almost too good. He didn't want to come like this, didn't want to—

Her tongue slicked over his tip, bathing the heated skin with her moisture.

He groaned in surrender. Not that he hadn't already given in to her but, oh hell...

He thrust a few times, the drag on his cock enticing in ways completely different than being encased in a woman's sex.

Which was the next stop on this erotic journey they'd just started. One he couldn't wait another second to get to.

"Carrie. Lie down."

She didn't obey right away. No, she licked him again, barely touching him with her tormenting tongue before she lay back on the bed and let her legs fall open. Lifting her foot, she trailed her toes from his thigh to his hip with unerring accuracy before moving between his legs and rubbing her big toe against his balls.

His groan echoed in the open loft and he grabbed her foot to hook her leg around his hips. Then he reached for her other leg and hiked it around his waist, remembering at the last second to grab a condom from the drawer in the bedside table.

Carrie watched his every move from between slitted lids, the smile on her lips a promise that he was about to have the best sex of his life.

With her long legs wrapped around his waist and her ass in one hand, he fitted his cock to her opening with the other and pushed inside.

God, she was wet and tight, and she moaned as if he were the best thing she'd ever felt. Arching her back, she threw her arms over her head and reached for the other side of the king-size mattress.

"So good," she murmured. "So good."

He worked his cock into her by increments, centimeters at a time, drowning in the sensation of flesh on flesh—wanting to thrust hard and fast but not sure she'd be able to take him all the way. Not to brag, but he was seven feet tall and well-proportioned.

"Carrie, are you okay?"

Her response was to arch her hips and take a few more centimeters with a throaty, "Mm hmm. I'm fine. I'm more than fine. Please, do me."

His balls tightened in anticipation. Christ, he was gonna come just from the sound of her voice.

No, not yet.

First, he had to get all the way inside her. He didn't know how long it took until he felt her fine hair mesh with his, but when he did, they both froze.

So damn good. And he hadn't started to move yet.

Obviously, she was thinking the same because she opened her eyes and held out her arms, her mouth curved in a sexy smile. She wanted him to come to her, to cover her with his body and he wasn't about to say no.

Careful not dislodge from her, he eased his knees onto the bed, scooting her forward so he could join her. The motion made them both groan, the anticipation building to an almost fever pitch.

A full foot taller than Carrie, he covered her completely, her head tucking under his chin, his body surrounding hers, pressing her into the bed.

He wondered for a second if he'd scared her when he heard her take in a sharp breath. But her moan and the rocking motion of her hips reassured him she was right there with him. And just as horny.

"Come on, babe," she said, "I want you to move. I *need* you to move."

"Don't worry. You'll get it."

As slowly as he could go, he pulled out, feeling every delicate ripple of her inner tissues. He wasn't aware he was holding his breath until he had to suck in air when he pulled completely free.

She immediately arched into him and he allowed her to take him back in. Slow. He wanted to take it slow, wanted her to beg.

He managed slow for a few minutes, an easy glide that made her writhe beneath him and cranked his blood pressure until his heart felt like a jackrabbit in his chest.

Still, he managed to submerge his need to pound into her. Until she slid her hands around his shoulders and down his back. Her nails took sharp little bites in his skin on the way down to his ass, where she pressed down with enough force to make him move.

Tilting her head up, she licked his throat then whispered, "Faster."

That one word was all it took. His body responded before his brain fully comprehended what she'd said.

He came up on his elbows and began to thrust, his hips pumping hard, her heels on his ass urging him faster. Every sound she made, every sigh, every moan, lit an answering fire in his gut that translated to tension in his balls.

Moving faster, he felt her legs creep higher on his waist, tilting her pelvis into him, opening her wider. A slight adjustment to his angle of penetration and she gasped.

Right there. That's where she needed the friction.

He wasn't going to come until he'd knocked her off the edge. That little bit of focus helped pull him back, helped him make sure he stroked the base of his cock against her clit.

She rewarded him with a loud gasp and the snap of her body against his as she came.

Her sheath clenched around him like a fist, milking him until the tension released in his balls and pumped his seed through his cock and into her.

Collapsing over her, breathing like a freight train, he pressed a kiss to her forehead and whispered, "Name's Tim. Nice to meet you."

Chapter Two

It took Carrie a few minutes to realize what the guy had said.

She was enjoying the afterglow. She'd never come that hard before. Kinda scrambled the brains.

So his name was Tim. Nice. Nice, normal name.

But why had he just introduced himself like she'd never asked his name before?

Had she been that drunk the night before?

Tim rolled to her side and she immediately missed his bulk surrounding her.

Wow, scary. She'd only known the guy... What? A couple of hours?

What the hell had she been drinking last night that—

Wait a minute. She hadn't gone out last night. She distinctly remembered going home because no one else had felt like going out. Most everyone at the office was sick.

She'd gone home, watched a little TV. She was working her way through the second season of *The X-Files*. Lots of great material in there for inspiration.

This morning, she'd gone to work and Bill had sent her out to get photos. For a Bigfoot spread.

Shaking her head, she sat up, inching away from him, more than a little thankful for the dark so he couldn't see her.

"Hey, you okay?"

Whoa, that voice sent shivers down her spine, so deep and sexy. But she had no idea why it sounded so familiar to her.

"Where am I?"

He didn't answer right away and she sucked her bottom lip between her teeth, chewing on the soft flesh. Maybe she didn't want to know.

"You're in my home. You're safe here, Carrie."

She felt safe. Still... "And where exactly did we meet?"

He sighed and the mattress moved as he rolled to the side of the bed and started to move around the room, opening and closing a drawer.

"I'm going to turn on a light, okay?"

"Uh, yeah. That's fine."

Considering how they'd just spent the past however many minutes, she shouldn't have been worried about her nudity.

And she forgot about it the moment he turned on the lights.

Holy hell, the guy was *big*. And she didn't just mean tall. He was perfectly proportioned—to be a freaking god.

He stared down at her from the side of the bed, one hand on his hip, not at all embarrassed by his nudity. His other hand held a t-shirt and a pair of boxer shorts, which she took, with her mouth hanging open.

She'd realized he had long hair but the dark had hidden the gorgeous mass of gold, brown and red waves. The shaggy lengths just reached his shoulders and again... Wow.

Broad and muscled but not overly so, this guy wasn't some angular long-distance runner or gangly basketball player. His golden skin gleamed in the dim glow of the lamp on the bedside table.

Letting her gaze drop even farther, she eyed his six-pack abs with something close to awe then her mouth went dry when she reached his groin.

She'd already known his sex was tremendous but she hadn't realized she'd want to immortalize it in stone. Or firm latex.

Sue her.

And his legs. Muscular thighs, shapely calves and huge feet.

Guess that myth was true. The size of a guy's feet and his, well... Yeah...

By the time she'd dragged her gaze back up to meet his eyes, his lips had quirked into a smile.

She glared at him even as she felt that tug of desire deep in her gut. "I didn't pick you up in a bar last night, did I?"

He shook his head, his expression clearing into something close to a blank slate.

"But I did wrap my car around a tree?"

He nodded. "Yeah. I didn't see you do it, but I heard. I found you passed out in the snow and brought you back here."

Her mouth opened for a second before she could put words together. "And decided you'd get a little nookie from the unconscious girl?" She pulled the oversized t-shirt over her head, a little freaked out, though she wasn't sure why. "Who *are* you?"

His face twisted in a contrite grimace. "Hey, I didn't want to take advantage of you. But you woke up, a little, uh…"

She couldn't believe he was too much of a gentleman to say she'd woken horny as hell.

"Well, that's mostly your fault." She felt inclined to point out. "You were naked and you smelled good and…and you were *hard*."

Surely she couldn't be held responsible for wanting him under those conditions.

His brows raised and those gorgeous lips kicked into a full-blown smile. Which made her hot for him and pissed off at him at the same time.

"Okay, I'll cop to all those."

Damn, the guy was so freaking *hot*. Which probably led him to believe he could get away with anything. Well, not with her. "Who the *hell* are you?"

"My name's Tim Sattazahn." He gestured around him, still looking a little sheepish, a little guilty. "This is my home. I own Outdoor Enterprises, a camping and wilderness business. I'm closed for the winter, though."

Okay, that didn't sound too bad. It sounded normal. But if the guy was a serial killer, of course he wouldn't say, "I'm a serial killer. Let me get out my chainsaw."

Her eyes narrowed and she tried on her most fierce expression. "Why'd you take off my clothes?"

Again, he looked abashed as he held out his hands, palms up. "They were wet and you were cold. It was the easiest way to warm you."

Okay, that sounded kind of rational, too. She felt her mouth purse into a thin little line as she thought about that.

"So," he asked, "what were *you* doing out here in the middle of nowhere in a snowstorm?"

Well, shit. How should she answer that one?

Most people, when she told them where she was employed, laughed in her face then asked what she really did. She'd grown a thick skin over the years but she didn't want this man to laugh at her.

Not that she was ashamed of her job, not in the least. Still…

Her chin tilted up. "I'm a writer."

He lifted one eyebrow at her. "Which doesn't explain why you were out here in the middle of a snowstorm."

She stuck her nose in the air, practically daring him to make some crack about women drivers and snow. "I'm out here for a story."

Now a wary look came into his eyes. "A story?"

"I work for a newspaper."

His gaze definitely went a little frosty on her and her reporter antenna pinged. Usually only people who had something to hide didn't like reporters. "So what story's so important to make you come out in a snowstorm for it?"

Good question. What would he say if she told him she was here to photograph Bigfoot?

Speaking of big feet…

She looked down. Damn, this man certainly proved that old chestnut about the size of a guy's feet indicating the size of his cock.

They had to be at least a fourteen or a fifteen, if not bigger.

Could he be the reason she'd been sent out here? Had someone gotten a quick look at him and thought…

No, that was just stupid. Yeah, the guy was tall but really, that was stupid.

Maybe she'd hit her head harder than she'd thought.

"Carrie?"

"Wait, how do you know my name?"

"I checked your driver's license." He held up a hand, for some reason drawing her gaze back to his exposed groin. The man was built *not* to wear clothes. "And before you complain, I just wanted to make sure you didn't have any medical conditions I needed to know about."

"I don't. I'm perfectly healthy." And so was he, if his physique and stamina were any indication. Speaking of stamina—

Jeez, she had to get him into clothing so she could think clearly. Obviously she should be angrier about him taking advantage of her.

Okay, maybe saying he'd taken advantage was a little harsh. He *had* tried to get her to stop at least twice.

Thank God she hadn't listened.

She held up her hand in classic stop position, though she didn't know why. "Look, could you put some clothes on? Please? Your nudity is making me nervous."

His smile lit his eyes. "Nervous, huh? Well, we certainly don't want that."

He turned and walked back to the chest of drawers against the far wall and she considered begging him to ignore her previous request and walk around naked all day.

The man had *the* most perfect ass. Lean and firm and rounded and—

She swallowed. Yeah.

Before she could completely embarrass herself and put her hands on that ass, he'd grabbed a pair of jeans out of a drawer and pulled them up those long legs.

He didn't bother with a t-shirt, though, and for that she again thanked that elusive Goddess of Hot Guys.

"So," he turned back to her, "since you're not going anywhere for a while because of the storm, you want something to eat?"

Come to think of it, she was kind of hungry. "It's still snowing?"

He nodded. "Hasn't stopped."

"Got any chocolate?"

* * * * *

Watching Carrie drink hot chocolate gave Tim a hard-on guaranteed to drive nails.

She didn't actually drink it. She licked at the marshmallows then lapped at the chocolate, her pink tongue mesmerizing him with thoughts of what she could do with it.

"This is really good." She practically purred, her eyes closed, hands wrapped around the mug. "I don't think I've ever had hot chocolate made from real chocolate bars. Where'd you learn to do that?"

"My mom. She's good in the kitchen." Which was a gross understatement. His mom was a wizard with chocolate, which was really saying something in his community. The Citeka loved their chocolate.

"Well, your mom knows her stuff." She gave the chocolate another lap and his cock twitched in his pants. The damn zipper was going to be imprinted on his flesh for sure.

He wanted her back in his bed. Wondered how long before he could make a move without her thinking he was taking advantage.

But he also wanted to know more about her.

"So, what paper do you work for?"

She looked him straight in the eyes. "The *Weekly News Journal.*"

Oh *shit.* Oh, no *fucking* shit. The fates wouldn't be that unfair, would they?

He tried to school his features into polite interest, instead of abject horror. "Um, not sure I'm familiar with that one," he lied.

Carrie didn't drop her gaze. "We cover news the other papers don't."

God damn, he *had* heard her right. He wanted to throw back his head and bellow. Damn it to hell and back again. Which deity had he pissed off lately?

It just wasn't fucking fair that the red-haired goddess wearing his shirt and nothing else was one of *those.*

Squashing a sigh, he prepared to have his hopes of doing her again crushed. "And what kind of news is that?"

Her chin lifted just a little bit higher, as if she were daring him to laugh. "Crop circles, UFO sightings, ghosts, out-of-the-ordinary stories."

He didn't laugh, couldn't find it in him to muster the strength. "Huh. That's...interesting."

She stiffened and set her mug on the counter. Very gently. "It *is* interesting. There's so much in the world we don't understand, so much that can't be explained by science." Then she shrugged and picked up her mug again. "But mainly, I'm in the entertainment field."

He blinked. Okay, not exactly what he'd expected to hear. "Entertainment?"

"Sure." Her slow smile had his blood chugging through his veins. "There's very real evidence for the existence of ghosts. UFOs? Not so much. I mean, I'm not arrogant enough to believe Earth is the only inhabited planet in the entire galaxy. But do I think people from other planets visit ours and kidnap people to probe them with steel rods?" She shrugged. "Not likely. Crop circles make good pictures but I've never come across one that couldn't be explained by a couple of kids and a little alcohol. Cryptozoology, now, that has some merits."

More than she knew. "How so?"

"The earth is a huge place. Scientists are finding new species every day. Of course there are going to be animals in the world we don't know about."

"So, you go around trying to take photos of the Loch Ness Monster and Bigfoot?"

She grimaced a little. "I've never been to Loch Ness. Do I think a dinosaur lives there? Not really. Would I love to go and be proved wrong? Hell yes. Do I think there's a huge man-ape running around the North American forests? No. I don't believe in Bigfoot. At least, not in some freak-of-nature missing link."

Well, thank God for small favors.

"But," she continued, "did you know that a race of red-haired giants once lived in the western part of the country?"

His heart sank farther toward his stomach with each word. "Uh…"

"There are several documented cases of seven- and eight-foot-tall skeletons found in caves in the West and… I'm boring you to tears, aren't I?"

No, unfortunately she wasn't. But what the hell could he say? "Not at all. I've never really given that kind of stuff much thought, though."

Christ, if he lied any more, his nose would start growing.

"Sorry. I get carried away with work sometimes." She let her gaze drift as she shook her head. "I enjoy it. I used to work for my dad. He's the managing editor of the *Harrisburg Daily*. My dad loves his politics. I think it's deadly dull and sucks out your soul after a while. We had a difference of opinion about that. Actually, we had several differences of opinion. So I left."

He knew how hard it was to leave your family and strike out on your own. "And decided you were really going to piss off your dad and work for the *Weekly News Journal*."

There was that smile again. The one that made him want to pick her up and throw her on his bed. If she didn't stop smiling, he was definitely going to have blue balls.

"Actually, no. I freelanced for a while but you can't make enough to pay the bills. Then I saw an ad in the classifieds for a staff writer at a weekly paper. I didn't really know what I was getting into at first. I just needed to pay my rent.

"My first assignment was an article on a haunted house in Oley. A ghost that played music all night and forced the homeowners to dance with him. Turns out the neighbors had outdoor speakers they forgot to turn off most nights. I had the best time writing that story. After that, I was hooked.

"Where else would I get to take mundane events like a flu epidemic or an overgrown dog running around someone's backyard and make them fantastic? I've been there going on three years now."

"Sounds like you love your job."

Her smile made his blood burn. "It's fun. It may not be my dad's idea of journalism, but there's got to be a balance between all the political bullshit and the misery, right?"

When she put it that way... "Yeah, I guess so. So, you were out here for a story? In the snow?"

"It wasn't snowing this much when I left. And by the time I realized it had turned into a blizzard, I was already here. I figured I'd just get the photos and get home."

"Photos of what?"

She waved a lazy hand as she took another sip of the chocolate. "The trees, the area. Any wildlife that may be around."

Damn, he knew where this was going but he couldn't stop himself from asking. "Wildlife?"

She sighed. "Bigfoot, okay. I'm here to do a story on Bigfoot."

Carrie couldn't tell by the look on Tim's face whether he wanted to laugh, sneer or shake his head.

She'd had her fair share of all three in the time she'd worked for the *Journal*.

Usually, she didn't give a rat's ass what other people thought. If they couldn't accept what she did as a legitimate form of entertainment, then they needed to loosen up or get a life. Or both.

Hell, many of the people who looked down on her job regularly devoured *US Weekly* and *In Touch*. Those weekly tabloids dished just as much pain and misery as her father's "respectable" daily.

"Bigfoot, huh?" Tim's tone was carefully modulated, revealing nothing about his thoughts. "Someone saw Bigfoot near here?"

She nodded. "Got a call yesterday. My editor wanted some live pictures of the area, since we're so close."

Stretching his long legs out in front of him, he crossed his feet and rested his hands on his naked, flat stomach.

Damn, the guy was sexy as hell. Even his feet turned her on. They were lean and long and... Oh, for chrissakes, she was lusting after his feet.

"So," he paused as if trying to find the right words, "you're looking for Bigfoot."

She almost sighed but caught it back just in time. "No. I told you, I don't believe in Bigfoot. But when my editor tells me to get live photos of the area for the pages next week, I do what he says."

Tim nodded, his expression thoughtful as he stared at her.

Did he think she was a nut case? Did he regret having sex with her?

Hell, she certainly hoped not. Because they were going to be seriously bored to tears if they were stuck in this cabin together until the snow let up and they didn't have sex to break up the monotony.

And she really, *really* wanted to have sex with him again.

She wasn't a slut. She chose men as carefully as she chose her hairstylist and she was damn picky about who cut her hair.

But she trusted her instincts and her instincts said this man was a keeper.

Hell, he could've taken advantage of her in so many different ways, it was scary to contemplate. Yet, he'd been the utmost gentleman. And he'd given her the best orgasm she'd ever had.

He nodded, as if agreeing with her unspoken determination and she became mesmerized by the slide of his beautiful hair on his shoulders. She'd never seen anyone with hair like that.

"Guess your photos are going to have to wait until we can get back to your car," he said. "Do you want to call your editor and tell him you're not going to make it back tonight?"

Damn, he was thoughtful too. If he was some nutcase, no way would he let her call anyone to tell them where she was. He had to be on the up-and-up. "Yeah, I would. Thanks."

"I've got a satellite phone hookup." He rose to walk to the counter where he grabbed a blocky-looking phone off the counter. "Out here I can't rely on regular phone lines or cell coverage."

Giving him a warm smile, she called the newsroom and spoke with her editor and explained the situation, reassuring Bill several times that she was safe. Maybe the guy did have a heart, after all. He even demanded she give him Tim's name and his address, which Tim supplied.

When she hung up, Tim was kneeling in front of the fireplace, tossing logs into the flames. Walking over to stand next to him, she marveled again at his size. The top of his head was nearly level with her chin. If he turned, he'd probably be able to put his mouth on her breasts.

Just the thought of his lips on her nipples made her thighs clench in anticipation.

"So, Tim, what are we going to do for the rest of the day?"

Good question, Tim thought, throwing another log on the fire. And a dangerous one.

Because what he wanted to do involved his bed, a can of whipped cream and her naked body.

Christ, was it possible to have an erection-induced heart attack?

He wanted this woman like he'd never wanted anyone else. The fact that he liked her made him want her even more.

Smart, self-deprecating and funny women turned him on like nobody's business. Throw in Carrie's red hair and awesome body and—*ding, ding, ding.* Jackpot.

He picked up another log, even though the fire was burning bright. "Um, I think I've got a few board games or a deck of cards around here somewhere. Unless you want to watch some TV?" It would run down the generator and he had a finite supply of gas but if that's what she wanted—

Her hand landed on his shoulder, winding a piece of his hair between her fingers. He'd been thinking about cutting it lately. The wavy, crazy-colored mass of it, combined with his height, made him too damn memorable. If he wanted to have a shot at fitting in out here, he'd have to get rid of it.

Of course, maybe he'd never be able to fit in anywhere but the small village where his parents and most of his family still lived. Citeka, Nevada, boasted less than five hundred inhabitants, most of those related through blood or marriage.

The village had been founded more than a hundred and fifty years ago, after their tribe had moved from its former home in the Pacific Northwest. It was located hundreds of miles from either Reno or Vegas and in an area no one willingly moved to.

Travelers didn't even pass through because the village wasn't located on any major highways. So they didn't get a lot of outsiders gawking. And calling tabloid newspapers.

Damn it, someone must have seen him out here and called the tabloid to report a Bigfoot sighting. Just because he hadn't seen anyone in the past few days didn't mean someone hadn't seen him.

How could he have been so careless?

"You have beautiful hair," Carrie murmured, sending shivers down his spine to his balls and his aching cock and bringing him back into the moment. "Did you get this from your mom or your dad?"

"My dad." Actually, all males in his family had variations on the same theme. His hair was more brown than his dad's, which was closer to Carrie's auburn.

Her fingers combed through the ends and, even though he was

done feeding wood into the fire, he stayed where he was.

"Do you have any brothers or sisters?" she asked.

"One of each."

"Younger or older?"

"I'm the oldest."

"Is your whole family so *tall*?"

He swallowed a bitter laugh at her innocent question. "Yeah, they are. What about you, Carrie?" He turned to stare up at her. "Where did you get that gorgeous red hair?"

Her smile made his gut twist. "My mom, though hers is steel gray now and just as beautiful."

Slowly he rose, catching her hand before she could retract it. She didn't pull away, just stared up into his eyes.

She shook her head. "I don't want to watch TV."

His mouth dried and he had to swallow to be able to speak. "Then what do you want to do?"

She lifted his hand to her breast, rubbing his knuckles over her pebbled nipple through his shirt. Her teeth bit into her bottom lip as she took a deep breath.

Okay, he could do that.

He lifted his other hand to join the first and watched her eyes flutter closed as her lips parted. Pinching her nipples through the soft cotton, he teased the already hard tips until she moaned.

She liked him to pinch hard rather than soft, to knead the firm mounds rather than caress. He'd learned that much about her already. He wanted to know everything.

Her head dropped back, exposing her throat and he angled his head so he could nip at the soft skin below her ear. She had cute ears, small and perfectly round, unmarked by piercings. She didn't have any other jewelry on her body except for a small silver ring on her right index toe that he'd only noticed a few minutes ago.

With his mouth still tasting her, he drew in a deep breath and noticed only the scent of vanilla lotion on her skin. She didn't wear any makeup, which she didn't need anyway.

Natural, fresh and refreshingly sexually open.

Was this his lucky day or what?

The answer was "Hell, yes" when she placed her hands on his hips and started a slow, sensual exploration of his skin. She touched every inch of exposed flesh she could reach, from his shoulders to his arms to his wrists. Her hands skimmed down his back to just above his jeans.

He groaned against her throat when her fingers slid around to the front, scratching lightly at the skin low on his stomach.

And when he felt her reach lower, his cock strained to break free of the waistband of his jeans. But still she didn't touch him.

Just when he thought he couldn't take it anymore, she slid her hands those few extra inches to the button on his jeans. But she didn't unbutton them.

He froze, waiting for her next move.

Which didn't come.

Instead, she tilted her head farther to the side and rolled her shoulder.

Ah. He strung kisses along her neck until he reached her jaw then followed the line of her jaw to her temple. Her hands responded by teasing his abdomen just above the waistband of his jeans.

Okay, she didn't want to play board games, but this game was even better.

Keeping one hand on her breast, he slid the other down her side and around the back to smooth over her ass. On the downward glide, he caught the fabric of the boxers she wore between his fingers and gave a good tug.

Her fingers slid back to the front and carefully worked open the button before easing down his zipper. She had to struggle a little to get it over his erection but finally she managed it without catching anything vital in those metal teeth.

To reward her, he kissed her forehead and shoved the boxers off her hips, drawing his hand around to the front to stroke through the fine hair between her legs.

It was her turn to shudder, pressing her face against his chest as her hands froze in the process of pulling his jeans off his hips.

He stilled his fingers.

"Two can play this game," she said.

"I thought we were."

He felt her smile brush against his chest, then her tongue slicked out to lap at his skin. A shiver rattled his body and his hands flexed on her breast and her mound.

And it wasn't a game anymore, unless she considered driving him out of his mind a game.

"Carrie."

He didn't know what else to say, only that he needed her to do something. Anything.

"Tim."

"I want your mouth on me."

"Where do you want my mouth?" Her voice flowed like warm oil over his skin. "Here?"

His breath stilled as her lips brushed across his right shoulder.

His fingers slid a little closer to her clit. "No."

"Here." Her mouth slid down to his nipple, her tongue flicking over the hard nub, making him groan at the sensation.

"On my cock."

"I think that can be arranged."

With a shove, she pushed his jeans as far down his legs as they could go. Then she wrapped one hand around his shaft while the other cupped his balls.

And went to her knees.

His head fell back as his hands gripped her shoulders. He didn't want to force her to do something she didn't want to do but—

Her mouth enclosed the tip of his shaft in moist heat, forcing a groan from deep in his chest. Fire shot from his balls, up his spine and into his head, where synapses in his brain began to spark.

She took him deeper in increments, working her way down his shaft with a lazy pace. Sweat beaded on his forehead when she finally reached the root and started to work her way back up.

Her tongue flicked over the head like a lash before she sucked hard. His groan echoed through the room as her hands caressed his balls with a light touch, a direct counterpoint to the fierce suction.

She worked him with her mouth, his brain going completely blank, able only to process pleasure.

When she finally released him, he took a deep breath and opened his eyes to find her staring straight into his.

Those beautiful green eyes broke his control and he grabbed her around the waist, pulling her up against him and smashing his lips down on hers.

She sighed into his mouth, as if she'd been waiting forever for him to kiss her.

He tore the boxer shorts off her legs then had to release her mouth to get her shirt off. Before the shirt hit the floor, he grabbed her close again, her warm skin so damn soft against his.

Lowering her to the floor, he laid her out on the plush rug in front of the fire. As she smiled up at him, she moved her hands to her breasts, cupping them and playing with the hard nipples.

Lust rode him hard and he stood to shed his pants, grabbing the condom from the pocket before tossing them aside. Then he dropped to his knees between the legs she spread for him.

Now sheathed, his cock pulsed in his hand and he clamped two fingers around the base to keep from coming.

She watched him, her eyelids lowering even more as her smile spread. *Witch*. She liked the effect she had on him. Frankly, so did he.

Without warning, he slid his fingers through her slit, making her moan. When he had the confirmation of her desire all over his fingers, he started working two fingers into her. Slow and easy, he thrust and retreated, watching her every expression. Her eyes closed on his first inward glide, her lips parting in a sensual sigh. Her back arched just the slightest bit, allowing him to go even deeper. Her sex felt like slick, warm satin pulsing around his fingers in an ever-increasing beat.

He pumped in and out, taking it slow, focusing her passion on the spot they were joined—at her pussy. His cock began to throb in time to his thrusts, an ache building in his balls.

Carrie arched with each invasion, her breathing harsh in the quiet room. The sound rasped against his nerves, stroked along his shaft and damn near caused him to hyperventilate.

Her fingers plucked at her hardened nipples. He nearly swallowed his tongue as he watched her play with herself, watched her hands squeeze and release then slide down her stomach. Her head rolled from side to side, a moan passing through those luscious lips.

She came without warning, eyes closed, her hands reaching for his wrists, trying to hold him in place. But he wouldn't let her. He kept pumping until he couldn't take it any longer and fell on her with a raging hunger.

Propping himself on his arms so he could watch her face, he pushed his cock into her incredibly tight pussy, her contractions clamping around him. She was so damn tight, he didn't think he was going to get all the way in before he came, but he couldn't stop.

In a few centimeters, out a few centimeters. In a little farther until finally he swore his cock touched her womb.

She moaned again, her eyes opening to look into his.

He had no defenses against the raw pleasure he saw on her face and let his hips slam back and forth, fucking her with a brutal strength that had her wrapping her legs around his waist and her hands around his wrists, bracing herself.

The earthy sounds coming from her mouth let him know he wasn't hurting her. In fact, she encouraged him to go faster with the beat of her heels against his ass.

His hips nailed her to the floor with each thrust, shooting wicked bolts of lightning up his spinal cord and into his brain. His synapses fried and his brain shut down so that all he knew was sex.

Carrie's musky scent, the sensation of his cock sliding in and out, the warmth. He wished he wasn't wearing the condom so he could feel her wetness against his skin.

Time lost all meaning as they lost themselves in the act, in each other.

His orgasm hit him as suddenly as hers had, his seed spilling from his cock, seeming to go on forever.

And a warmth that had nothing to do with sex followed on its heels.

With the final spasms, he let his body cover hers completely. Her arms wrapped around him and she sighed into his chest.

And fell asleep.

Chapter Three

Tim woke, wrapped around Carrie.

He'd carried her to the loft after that last bout of sex, crawled in bed beside her and went lights out.

Boom, boom, boom.

He sucked in a breath.

What the hell was that?

The sound came again and he thought the wind must have kicked up and was banging a tree limb against the wall.

He hoped it didn't wake...

Wait. *Shit.* Someone was pounding on the front door.

Tim rose, grabbing a pair of gym shorts from the pile of clean clothes on the chair next to the bed, trying not to disturb Carrie who was still out like a light. He took the stairs two at a time and skidded to a stop before the door. Checking the sidelight next to the door, he nearly groaned at the sight of the people standing on the porch.

Shit. *Shit, shit, shit.*

He ripped open the door before they started pounding again.

"Damn, Andy, what the hell are you doing here?"

His cousin stood on the porch, staring at him from beneath the hood of his white coat. His pale gray eyes widened and Tim felt guilt twist in his gut.

"Nice to see you, too, Tim. Guess that 'Come by and visit anytime' was bullshit, huh?"

Yeah, he was an ass. He shook his head and waved the pair in. "Shit, I'm sorry. You caught me at a bad time. Hey, Fry, what's up?"

The other man shrugged his shoulders, the humps on his back moving up and down under his coat. "Not much. Cold as a bitch out there today. At least it stopped snowing."

Fry started to unzip his coat but stopped midway, his nose twitching. "Uh, you got company, Tim?"

Andy paused for a second as he picked up the scent then laughed, a short bark of sound. "Hell, now I know why you're not happy to see us." He pushed his hood down and his white-blond hair fell out and around his shoulders. "Dude, you get lucky today?"

Tim gave him the finger. "None of your damn business. But you can't be here when she wakes up."

Andy's pale eyebrows rose. "She's one of them? I thought you swore off that flavor after Jenny."

"She's nothing like Jenny." *The bitch.* "But if she gets a load of you two, she's gonna put two and two together and come up with front-page news."

Andy hung his coat next to Carrie's on a wall hook and ran his hands through his hair, bending down to take off his boots. "We just need to hang out for a few hours then we'll go."

Tim glanced at Fry, who shrugged and looked apologetic. As opposed to Andy, who just looked amused. And a little worried.

Tim got a bad feeling. "What's going on, Andy? And don't tell me you just decided to make a trip halfway around the world to say hi."

His cousin's long legs ate the space between the door and the fireplace in two strides and he stuck his hands close to the screen to warm them, even though Tim knew he couldn't be cold. Hell, the guy lived high in the Himalayan Mountains most of the year. This twenty-degree weather should be subtropical for him.

When Andy didn't answer, Tim turned to Fry, who was just hanging up his coat. Flapping his blue-tinted wings a couple of times to stretch them, he turned to Tim and shrugged. His ears, the pointed tips clearly visible through his tousled black hair, twitched.

"Sorry, Tim," Fry said. "We picked up a SPAz tail in Jersey. We think we lost him somewhere in Kutztown, but we're not sure."

Tim's temples began to thump. Great, just fucking great. The members of the Society of Paranormal Anomalies, which Tim's community had given the unflattering and completely appropriate nickname of SPAz many years ago, were first-rate pains-in-the-ass.

Tim scrubbed at his eyes, trying to ease the headache he felt building. "Christ, Andy. You don't know how much of a bad time this is."

His cousin shrugged. "I must have been in the wrong place at the wrong time. I didn't even know I was going to pick up Fry in England when I started out from home. I was gonna hang out in Ireland for a while but Fry contacted me and let me know he was in London. We decided to hop the Atlantic, hang out with you for a while then head up to the Mystyk Bar in Tioga. I only noticed the damn tail when we were halfway to Reading. They must've gotten a tip from someone at the airport."

"Hell, I'm not angry with you, Andy. But Carrie...well, she..."

"Doesn't know who you are?" Andy snorted. "No shit."

Tim sighed again. "No, I mean she's one of them."

Andy's perplexed expression would have been funny any other time. "You mean she's like Fry? Hell, buddy, if I'd known you had a thing for wings, I would have hooked you up with Gizelle years ago."

And that would have been much easier, wouldn't it? To fall for a woman from the Fringe.

"That's not what I mean."

Andy frowned. "Then what—" His eyes widened. "Oh, you have *got* to be kidding me? She's a *SPAz*?"

"No. Worse." He paused then bit the bullet. "She works for the *Weekly News Journal*."

Andy's mouth dropped open for at least fifteen seconds before he started to laugh. "Oh, you are so *fucking* screwed, cuz."

Yeah, he was. Totally.

Because, from behind him, he heard Carrie gasp.

* * * * *

There was no way she was awake.

Carrie figured she was having a dream because Tim was standing in his living room talking to a Yeti with long, blond hair and a winged Mothman.

Except the Yeti was no ape man and Mothman had the face of an English fairy, all sharp angles and points. And wings.

And the Yeti kind of looked like Tim. Yeah, there definitely seemed to be a family resemblance in the deep-set eyes, the high cheekbones and the square jaw.

Damn. She must have hit her head harder than she'd thought in the accident. And she definitely needed a vacation. Her job had finally started to get to her.

"Carrie?"

"Uh huh."

She heard Tim say something else but she couldn't take her eyes off those wings. They must be attached to the tight cotton sweater the guy wore. They couldn't be real.

But how the hell was he making them flap? And why the hell would he be wearing them?

Walking over to the guy, she twirled her finger in the air and damn, if the guy's mouth didn't quirk up at the corners before he did a slow turn, stopping to give his wings a kind of a preening flutter when he had his back to her.

Nope, those suckers weren't attached to the sweater. They actually poked through perfectly made slits in the fabric. They weren't all that big, each only about two feet across and maybe that long again. And they were blue. Actually, they were the exact shade of the sweater he was wearing.

He was a few inches shorter than she was and he looked tiny next to the other new guy.

The blond giant stared down at her.

"Hi." Blondie held out his hand. "I'm Andy. This is Fry."

She took his hand, wondering when she was going to see a bug-eyed alien or the Loch Ness monster walk by. "Hi back. Carrie Benton."

"Nice to meet you."

Mothman held out his hand and she took it. Felt real enough. Warm, soft skin. "Hello, Carrie." Faint trace of an accent, a bit like Scotty on *Star Trek*. Did that make him Irish? Scottish?

When he released her hand, she waggled her index finger in the general direction of his shoulders. "Those wings are great. How did you make those?"

The guy smiled, showing off shiny bright teeth and two pointed fangs. Not huge vampire fangs, just sharply pointed canines. Wow, he really went all out. Did he have those filed or did he glue them on?

He'd make a great cover for the *Journal*. She wondered if he'd let her photograph him.

Not that she believed he was a real fairy. There were no such things. This guy just had a little too much money and way too much time on his hands.

Still... She walked around to check out his wings again.

"Carrie?"

She didn't bother to glance up at Tim, just gave him a distracted

"Hmm?"

"You okay, babe?"

She smiled. "Fine. These are just too cool. How do you make them move?"

When Fry didn't answer, she glanced at him. He stared at her with an enigmatic smile. Like he was trying to tell her something.

She blinked.

No. There was just no way. No way in hell.

"Carrie?"

She glanced over at Tim, who looked a little green around the gills, his dark eyes shadowed.

And she was struck again by how tall he was. How tall both he and Andy were.

Her gaze narrowed and blurred as she continued to stare.

God...damn. No, she really must have messed up her head. They looked...like...

Oh, hell to the no. That was just whack.

"Tim?"

He sighed. "Yeah, babe?"

She tried. She really did. But she just couldn't get her mouth to form the words.

Instead, she shook her head and swore she felt a few marbles roll.

Tim walked over to her, put one large hand on her shoulder and squeezed. Heavy, warm. That hand had done amazing things to her body.

His eyes were such a warm brown, soothing and sexy at the same time.

If she was a fanciful person, she'd say she was half in love with the guy. She wanted to smile every time she looked at him.

But she wasn't in love with him. She couldn't be. She didn't do love at first sight. She'd been a reporter too long to believe in something as magical as that.

And he wasn't...couldn't be...

"Tim, I think... I think my job's going to my head." She tried to laugh but it sounded strained. "Maybe I hit my head harder than I thought because I just had the weirdest idea."

"Uh, Tim," Andy said, "your girl's got that look on her face."

Yeah, unfortunately, Tim had to agree. That look said her gears were working. Carrie was a bright woman. Too bright to let herself believe Fry's wings were real. But smart enough to want to figure out how he was making them move. And he knew she wouldn't let it go. She'd have Fry stripped out of his sweater in five seconds flat to find out exactly what she wanted to know.

And Fry would give it to her, if only for the pleasure of watching her realize those wings were real.

Then she'd take one more look at him and Andy and put two and two together and get Sasquatch.

When she did, would she still want him?

Or would she run screaming, calling him a freak all the way back to her office? When she got there, would she talk herself down, laugh about it, laugh about him? Then write up some outlandish story in her newspaper about her illicit love affair with Bigfoot?

"Carrie, are you okay?"

Now she turned to him and her expression told the whole story.

"His wings are real." Her tone was factual. Not even a hint of a question.

Tim thought about lying. Didn't want to, not to her. He nodded. "They are."

"And you two," she wiggled a finger back and forth between him and Andy, "you're related."

"We're cousins." Which was true. Tim's mom's sister had married Andy's dad. The Yeti and Citeka tribes did a lot of intermarriages. They had common ancestors, going back several centuries.

Their family trees looked more like an English royalty chart.

Her eyes narrowed. "And where did you say you're from?"

"Western Nevada."

She turned to Andy. "And you?"

Andy paused for a few seconds. "Nepal."

She nodded and her gaze arrowed back to Tim's. "Wow." Her rueful smile grew slowly and, as it did, Tim's heart sank. "Guess I owe my editor twenty bucks. I bet him there was no such thing as Bigfoot."

Carrie couldn't believe how easily all the pieces fit together and how easy it was for her to make the leap from skeptic to believer.

Of course, Tim did nothing to abuse her of the idea. He just stood there staring at her.

Andy was Yeti. Fry was a fairy. And Tim was…Bigfoot.

She wondered if he called himself that or if there was a more PC term—

No. *Great freaking Christ, no.*

Jesus, she was just as nuts as the people who wore tinfoil hats so aliens couldn't read their minds.

Tim wasn't some huge, hairy ape loping around the forest, impregnating rednecks and beating on idiots eating jerky.

There were no such beings as Bigfoot or Yeti or fairies. Logically, there was an explanation for the out-there conclusion she'd leaped over a crevasse to get to.

She looked up—and up—at Tim. His grim expression made her stomach clench. And not in the good way it had earlier.

"Tell me I'm wrong."

She couldn't form the words, couldn't make herself say, "Bigfoot."

Tim didn't say anything. Neither did Andy or Fry. They all just stood there, staring at her.

"Holy shit." Her eyes widened. "Holy shit. No wonder you look like you're gonna throw up."

Because he was nuts, that's why.

Tim started to shake his head. "Carrie—"

"No, wait." She held up one hand like a traffic cop. "Don't say anything. Let me… Just give me…a minute."

"Carrie, we need to talk."

She looked deep into his eyes, trying to will him to tell her the truth. Or convincingly lie to her. "Are you really going to tell me you're Bigfoot?"

He didn't smile, his expression showing nothing. "No."

She sighed, relief pouring over her like a waterfall. "Oh, thank G—"

"But…you remember those red-haired giants you say lived in the Western desert?"

Her mouth dropped open but she couldn't make a sound.

"I'm one of them."

She didn't say anything for a full thirty seconds, her mind a complete void. "You're an ancient giant?"

His lips in no way indicated a smile. "The group of humans who became the American Indians crossed a land bridge from Asia a millennia ago. Our tribe arrived then, as well. The Citeka, what we call ourselves, are an offshoot of Andy's Himalayan tribe, the Yeti. Most of my tribe lives in Nevada in a remote village, where we moved after leaving the Pacific Northwest. We don't get many visitors and we tend not to move around too much because, well…" He made a sweeping motion with his hands. "We're kind of noticeable."

Tim paused, as if trying to gauge her reaction but she just knew there was more so she raised her eyebrows and waited.

With a sigh, he finally continued. "We're pretty self-sufficient and most of us are gifted with an artistic gene. We make a lot of money creating artwork for galleries and high-end boutiques and designer showcases. But…we also make a fortune propagating the Bigfoot legend."

He looked completely serious even though she knew he had to be kidding.

"Bigfoot." Her tongue could barely make the word. "As in big, hairy ape-like creature with huge feet." Her gaze automatically dropped to Tim's large feet for a brief second and she just shook her head. "I'm sorry but even if I saw you walking through the forest at a distance, I'd still know you were a man and not…not…"

"A monster? A freak of nature?" Tim sighed. "We're not. But…we do have special, uh—"

"Hey, Tim, maybe we just oughta show her."

The sly amusement in Andy's voice made her eye him with apprehension. And more than a little challenge.

"And what exactly would you show me?"

Tim drew in a deep breath then held it for a few brief seconds as he felt the air in the room crackle with the electric sensation of impending magic.

And it was magic, a magic handed down through the ages. A magic lost to everyone but the few scattered tribes of the Fringe.

Normals knew of them only as myth. The faerie folk. The Vampyr. The witches.

The shapeshifters.

In the blink of an eye, Andy was gone and in his place stood a huge, shaggy, grayish-white bear. He looked nothing like the grotesque pictures people created of the infamous Yeti. He looked like a bear, except with a more human-looking face.

Nearly eight feet of soft fur, powerful muscle and fearsome teeth. Which he bared at Carrie in a smile right before he made a courtly bow.

He looked so much like a trained circus animal, Tim nearly laughed. But he couldn't quite get his vocal cords to cooperate.

Because Carrie made a sound halfway between a squeak and a yelp before she fell silent with her mouth hanging open. She stared at

Andy, wide-eyed and shocked.

But not afraid.

She'd already started to reach for him but her hand paused in the space between them. As if she needed permission to touch him.

Andy reached out his paw to meet her halfway and she drew in a deep breath when she touched his fur.

"Holy shit."

Tim braced himself for the inevitable screaming and running in fear most people did when faced with something magical and completely out of their comfort zone.

Of course, Carrie wasn't most people.

She turned to him, her cheeks flushed and eyes bright. "Can you do that too?"

His eyes narrowed, watching her for any sign of fainting. "Yes."

"Will you show me?"

He stared at her for a brief second, trying to debate all the angles.

She'd already seen Andy change and she seemed to be over her initial shock. And unlike in the movies, there wasn't any gross bone cracking or shedding of skin. It was pure magic.

But would she still want him after—

Oh hell, what did it matter at this point?

With a thought, he released the magic held in his very cells and let it transform his body into that of the reddish brown bear he'd lived with since he'd been a child. He could honestly say he loved his form, loved the strength and his glossy fur.

Loved the magic he'd been born with.

As he watched, Carrie sucked in a deep breath, her eyes wide.

Then she reached for him. Her hand paused for a brief second before she settled it over his forearm and stroked down to his hand.

Her touch felt wonderful against his fur but he knew how much better it felt against his skin and he shifted back into his human body, exactly as he'd been before he'd shifted.

She didn't pull away. She let her hand settle once again on the skin of his arm.

"That… That was…" She shook her head, blinking up at him.

"Andy's tribe has been perpetuating the Yeti myth for a thousand years." He moved his arm but only enough that he could lace their fingers together and hold her in place. "My tribe's only been doing it for a couple centuries. But it makes us a decent amount of money. The stories grew out of Western settlers catching sight of us in the forests.

It started as a way to keep outsiders away from our lands but when the Patterson film was released, we saw how much money there was to be made from the legend so we figured why not? Besides, it's harmless."

"And it's fucking hilarious." Andy had reverted back to his natural state. "Normals are just too much fun to play with. Y'all are pretty gullible."

Carrie frowned as her hands went to her hips as she stared up at Andy. "Gullible?"

"Don't get your panties in a twist, sweetheart." Andy patted her on the shoulder. "Most Normals can't see beyond the nose on their faces. If they can't touch it or explain it using science, well then, they think it can't exist, which is a damn shame, if you ask me. They miss out on so many wonders of the world."

Her head tilted to the side, her eyes narrowing. "So you taunt them?"

"We have our fun, yeah." Andy mimicked her pose. "You Normals make it so damn easy. All we have to do is walk upright through a few backyards and your people fall all over each other to tell the tabloids. Christ, the National Geographic Channel spends a mint on documentaries about Bigfoot and the Loch Ness Monster every year. Of course, we usually have a hand in making those shows. Bet you didn't know that, did you?"

Carrie blinked and her mouth opened then shut with a snap.

Andy just shook his head. "And you're all too willing to feed the frenzy, aren't you? You must have felt so superior to all those idiots who believe in people like us."

Carrie turned to face Tim again, her beautiful eyes sparkling. He swore he could see the gears turning in her brain. This was *so* not good. "So Fry's wings are real and you just turned into a bear?"

Tim's sigh held a note of resignation. "Yeah."

She swallowed and he could see the excitement she was trying to contain written all over her face. "Holy shit."

Tim just shook his head. "We call ourselves the Fringe. Fry's people are members. So are mine and Andy's."

"And Fry's a fairy."

"We call ourselves Fae," Fry chimed in, fluttering his wings for full effect. "You can call me whatever you like, sweetheart."

Whoa. Just…whoa.

Carrie's head buzzed with thoughts, images. Cutlines. Story ideas. Headlines.

"Does this mean aliens are among us? Bat Boy? Chupacabra?"

Tim's expression never changed. "I've never met Bat Boy."

Holy shit.

Holy freaking shit!

She'd crashed into the biggest story of her life. A story bigger than the *Weekly News Journal*. Bigger than the *Harrisburg Daily*. This was *New York Times* big. *Washington Post* big.

Pulitzer *freaking* Prize.

Her father would bow at her feet in awe.

And if she went public with it, she'd expose Tim, his family and his friends to the unwanted scrutiny of the entire world. And make his life a living hell.

She blinked up at him. "Tim, I—"

"Oh, *fuck*."

Carrie turned in time to see Andy make a beeline for the door. Throwing it open, he ran out into the snow. A flash of dark green streaked by the front window and she hurried to the door to see what was going on.

By the time she got there, Andy held someone three feet off the ground by the back of a forest camouflage coat. Squealing like a stuck pig, the man wore huge, round glasses that would have made him look like an insect if it weren't for his all-too-human expression of abject fear.

"Well, well, well." Andy turned the guy backward and forward as if he were inspecting a side of beef. "Looks like I caught a SPAz. My lucky day. I was just starting to get hungry."

Andy bared his teeth at the guy, setting off another round of squeals and Carrie rolled her eyes at Andy's over-the-top antics. How could anyone think the guy was serious?

Of course, if that weasely-looking guy had seen everything...

The SPAz shook and shivered and generally looked like he was about to be eaten. Yeah, he'd seen what she'd seen.

"So you wanna tell me who you are and what you're doing creeping around out here?" Andy shook his head and gave the guy a shake as well. "And don't be stupid and lie. Of course, you were stupid enough to wear forest cammie in the snow. Jesus, did you think you wouldn't stick out?"

"You c-c-can't h-h-hurt me." The man swung his gaze around at all of them, his pupils so dilated, she would have felt sorry for the guy—*if* he hadn't had that camera in his hands. "My f-f-friends know where I am. If I don't return, they know where to l-l-look for me."

"Yeah, but they won't find you." Andy bared his teeth again, straight and pearly white, though he did have rather elongated incisors. "At least, not all of you."

The guy paled even more, clutching his camera to his chest, his knuckles white with strain.

Carrie walked over to him, wrestled the camera away and started to flip through the digital pictures, her heart sinking as she realized he had pictures of Tim. Before and after his amazing change.

Hell. Even though the quality wasn't great, Tim's face was clearly recognizable right up until the moment he became a bear. And she could still see a little bit of Tim in the bear's eyes.

Her heart pounded against her ribs like a trapped bird.

She dropped the camera and brought her boot heel down on it, smashing it with a satisfying crunch as the man gave a girly squeal of protest.

Her dream of breaking this story was just that.

A dream.

* * * * *

Fry and Andy bundled the SPAz into Andy's rental SUV and drove off through the snow.

Tim knew Andy hadn't been serious about harming the guy. Once Andy used his own brand of inherent magic and wiped the guy's memories, he'd be harmless.

Now Tim watched Carrie as she just stared at him.

"I should be able to get you home now, if you want to go." The snow had stopped as abruptly as it had started and he'd be able to get her home safely in his Range Rover.

Not that he wanted her to go. He wanted her to stay.

He wanted her to *want* to stay.

"Can we just...talk a few minutes?" She looked at the sofa. "Just sit?"

Because he was an idiot, he waved her to the couch then sat on the chair opposite. He wanted to be on the cushion next to her but if he sat that close, he'd want to do more than just sit there.

Hell, he wanted more than one night with her.

And he knew that was out of the question.

He should take her memories of her time with him. Should but...

He was an idiot. He wanted her to remember him, to think about him.

Damn it to hell.

He'd have to think about moving. At least temporarily. His parents would be happy to see him. He could stay with them in Nevada for a while.

But… Damn it, he didn't want to leave. He liked it here. He'd never been much of an artist, unlike most of his family, and he made a decent living with his outdoor business during the other three seasons to live comfortably in winter. He liked the area and he liked the fact his family wasn't breathing down his neck at all times.

He wanted Carrie to say, "Don't worry, Tim. I'll keep your secret. I'll never tell a soul."

He wasn't even sure why he'd told her the truth. They could have lied, could have told her Fry's wings were fake and never let her see his and Andy's transformations.

But he hadn't wanted to lie to her.

She started to blink, as if holding back tears but she didn't cry. Instead, her chin went up and her mouth flattened into a straight line.

"Aren't you going to ask me not to do it?"

He continued to stare at her.

Her eyes narrowed as her hands clenched into fists on her lap. "So, you've already tried and convicted me? You're convinced I'm going to rat you out, aren't you?"

No, he wasn't. But… She was what she was. She was a journalist. Yes, she worked for a newspaper most people thought of as entertainment but even if she wrote half of what she'd seen today, there were enough people like the SPAz group out there to make his and his family's and friends' lives more precarious.

Tim shook his head. "Not at all. I like you, Carrie." Probably more than he should, considering. "And I don't want to guilt you into this decision. I think it'd probably be better if we had a little space to work this out. You're a journalist. I just dropped the story of your life into your lap. You need to make your own decision. I don't want to influence you."

But he hoped like hell that she wasn't going to break his heart.

Carrie couldn't decide whether she was pissed off, shocked or hurt.

Probably a combination of all three.

As she stood there and continued to glare up at the seemingly most perfect man in the world, she thought, *Of course he's a magical Bigfoot.*

Maybe she should consider herself lucky that she hadn't crashed into the forest of the Big Bad Wolf.

She'd never gotten the whole werewolf thing. She'd never read the obscenely popular series of books but if she'd have to choose between Team Edward and Team Jacob, she'd probably have to go with bloodsucker over canine. Dogs shed and she hated to sweep. Vampires didn't leave sparkles on your couch.

At least, she didn't think they did.

"So you're just going to drive me home and hope I don't tell the world, oh, by the way, Bigfoot and Yeti are real and I can introduce you to them?"

She wanted a response from Tim, any indication of his feelings but he continued to stand there looking at her.

And she couldn't read him. She had no idea what he was thinking.

Maybe he just wanted to be rid of her. Maybe she'd been completely wrong about him and now that he'd had sex with her, he didn't want her around anymore and this was a convenient way of making her be the bad guy and storm out in a rage.

"No, I'm going to drive you home and let you think about what you've seen."

"So I can do what with it?"

There, finally a crack in his outward composure. She swore she saw frustration flash through his eyes.

"I don't know, Carrie. Why don't you tell me what you think you can do with the information? Do you honestly think if you write our little…encounter up as a story for your rag that anyone will believe you?"

Her gaze narrowed as she bristled outwardly, although she sometimes called the *Weekly News Journal* the same thing. "Did you just call my newspaper a rag?"

His short, indrawn breath made her cover a quick satisfied smile. He thought he'd hurt her feelings. And if he just wanted to get rid of her, he wouldn't care.

"No… Well, yeah, I did but I didn't…" He scrubbed a hand through his hair in frustration, making the muscles of his arms bunch and flex as her mouth watered. "Damn it, Carrie. Just get your stuff. I'm taking you home."

She stuck her nose in the air. "And what if I don't want to go yet?"

"Why wouldn't you? Don't you have some story about some 'hairy ape'," he threw her own words back at her, "to write about?"

"Maybe I'd rather soothe your ruffled fur first?"

The look on his face was priceless, she decided. And he probably hadn't even caught her little pun about fur, which she thought was pretty damn inspired, if she did say so herself.

"What… Why would you want to do that?"

He looked genuinely confused and she wanted to cup that gorgeous chin in her hands and plant her lips over his.

She'd admit to being somewhat—okay maybe more than somewhat—shocked at the fact that this man was a shapeshifter. That he could become something else. It should have made any normal person scream like a little girl and run for the hills.

So maybe she wasn't all that normal.

Maybe she was just a little bit off.

But Tim was something special. Not just because of *what* he could do but *who* he was.

A great guy.

One she wanted more with each passing second.

So she wrapped a hand around his neck and pulled his head down until she could reach his lips to kiss him.

At first, he froze, gave her no response at all. His lips remained closed against hers and he didn't reach for her like he had before. He didn't wrap his arms around her and draw her closer against that gorgeous, hard body.

But she wasn't giving up. She let her tongue slide against the seam of his lips, licking, begging for entrance.

He shuddered at the touch and she felt his hands brush against her sides before grabbing her by the shoulders…

And holding her away from him.

"So now I'm a novelty fuck, right, Carrie?"

Her mouth dropped open in shock. "A novelty fuck? What the freaking hell is a novelty fuck?"

"I'm different. Some women get off on that."

Her lips parted to tell him he was freaking clueless about women if he thought she wanted him just because of what he could do. If anything, she should be hauling ass out of here.

Then she took a good look at him, at the expression in his eyes.

"Wait. You knew someone like that, didn't you?"

His head tilted back and his mouth flattened even more. He didn't need to answer. She could read it in his eyes.

"What a *bitch*."

He watched her for a second before nodding. "Yeah, she was."

"How did she find out about you?"

"I stupidly told her."

"You're not stupid."

Her immediate defense of him made the hard line of his mouth soften just a little bit. "No, maybe naïve would be a better word to describe my relationship with Jenny. I met her at a Fringe bar. She knew the scene, knew a few mutual acquaintances. What I didn't know was that she needed a shapeshifter for her belt."

"You mean... Geez, what a slut!" Then she realized what he wasn't saying. "Wait... You think I want you now because I know *what* you are? That that's the only reason I want you?"

He dropped his gaze for a brief second and when his returned to hers, she swore she felt the burn of it inside. "I don't honestly know what you want, Carrie. And I don't think you do either."

Chapter Four

"What the hell are you still doing here, Care? Go the fuck home already."

Bill Dailey dropped into the chair at the opposite cubicle in the offices of the *Weekly News Journal*, gnawing, as always on a toothpick. At forty-five, his dark good looks had weathered, making the man even more handsome than he'd been in his younger days. Not that Carrie had ever considered dating him.

The guy was married to the paper. And to his toothpicks. Bill had quit smoking nearly five years ago but he couldn't seem to quit chewing the picks down to splinters.

One of these days, he was going to choke on the damn things.

Carrie sighed as she minimized the story on her desktop. Glancing at the clock on the far wall of the newsroom, she realized it was close to eight p.m. and no one else remained on the floor.

"I'm working," she said. "What's your excuse?"

"When I signed my soul to this paper, they chained me to my desk. I didn't see that clause in your employment contract."

Damn, the man had a devastating smile. Too bad he barely ever used it when he held court at his u-shaped desk at the rear of the room. One side held a thirty-inch screen where he oversaw layout. Paper covered the opposite side—page proofs, article drafts, photo proofs. The last side, the one facing the newsroom, would have put a candy store to shame.

The joke was that the candy drew in unsuspecting prey then Bill ensnared them in his web and devoured them.

It was true the *Journal* had a high turnover rate among staff, though honestly, that wasn't all due to Bill's usually gruff nature. Some writers just didn't have the talent for making the impossible seem probable. Or at least amusing.

Bill was a damn good editor. He had awards filling his desk drawers from stints at the *Philadelphia Inquirer*, *Star Tribune* and *St. Petersburg Times*. As a former investigative reporter, he'd broken major political scandals and exposed police corruption while being able to bring a reader to tears with a column about a little girl selling cookies to raise money for her wheelchair-bound big brother.

Sometimes, though, even he couldn't save a story from the writer's inability to grasp the finer points of aliens in the White House. Little green aliens.

When she didn't respond to his last joke—which she really hoped was a joke—his gaze narrowed. "You sure nothing happened while you were at that guy's house over the weekend? You've been awfully quiet the past two days."

Because she'd been waging a battle she couldn't win, no matter how she looked at it. If she wrote the story that'd fallen in her lap and published it—whether in the *Journal* or in the *New York* freaking *Times*—she knew she'd never have a chance in hell with Tim again.

But every journalistic instinct in her clawed at the chance to write an article that could change the world.

She shook her head. "No, nothing happened. The guy was a complete gentleman. I slept on his couch Friday night and was home in my own bed Saturday. End of story."

Only, she didn't want it to be.

Tim had driven her home late Saturday afternoon, right after their little talk. He'd retrieved her cameras from her car, had even stopped for her to get a few shots of the snow-covered forest.

Neither of them had said much on the car ride, the awkward silence filled with unspoken desire and unanswered questions.

And when he'd pulled up in front of her modest townhome in Shillington, she hadn't known what to say so she'd kissed him and run. Like the coward she was.

She'd spent Sunday morning writing an article to go along with her gorgeous photos. An article that had just made it into this week's edition, published today.

She's spent the rest of Sunday researching, amazed at how much actual fact about the Fringe was out there for anyone to find. None of it, of course, from respected sources.

Geez, the story she could write…

"Bill, have you ever *not* written a story because of how it would affect the people involved?"

Bill's blue eyes narrowed on her as he leaned back in his chair. "I take it you're not talking about a story for the *Journal*. 'Cause you know what we write about isn't real, right? It's for entertainment purposes only."

The *Journal* had that disclaimer buried in the masthead, right under who to contact about sales.

And on any given day, Carrie believed that wholeheartedly.

But today…

"Have you?" she pushed.

Something passed through Bill's eyes, something sad. "No, I haven't. But that was a long time ago and I've learned my lesson. Some stories aren't meant to be printed. But that doesn't mean you shouldn't write them."

* * * * *

"Damn, man, if you're going to mope, move the hell to another table. You're bringing us all down and scaring away the ladies."

Andy just laughed when Tim gave him the finger. He, Andy and Fry had been holding up the bar at the Mystyk club, just outside of Wellsboro in Tioga County, since Tim had arrived Wednesday afternoon. He'd been sick of prowling his own home and had needed a change of scenery.

He'd thought spending time with other Fringe dwellers, people he knew and who knew him, would make him feel better.

So far, only the alcohol had made him feel better.

He was feeling no pain at the moment. Tequila was his new best friend.

"I'm not moping, asshole." Well, maybe he was a little but no way would he cop to it. Christ, he wanted to see Carrie again, which didn't make a damn bit of sense. "Hell, I didn't know her long enough to be moping. Not even twenty-four hours."

"And yet here you are," Andy said. "Moping like a five-year-old who had his favorite toy taken away. Why don't you just put yourself out of your misery and call her, you sorry SOB. You know you want to. And for what it's worth, I don't think she's anything like Jenny."

Andy's quietly sincere statement made Tim stare at his cousin. "Did you *not* read that article in the *Journal*?" He picked up the offending tabloid and shook it in the vicinity of Andy's face. Or at least, what he thought was the vicinity of Andy's face since he was seeing two of them at the moment. "She practically foamed at the mouth about how Bigfoot saved her from a car crash and nursed her back to health."

"Dude, the woman has a job, which she does amazingly well, if you didn't happen to notice. I laughed out loud reading it. That's some skill there. But only a complete idiot would believe that story was true."

"The article was rather humorous," Fry added. "I must admit I found the entire edition amusing."

Tim just shook his head. "Have you both gone off the deep end? She used me. Just like Jenny."

Andy snorted. "Carrie is nothing like that crazy bitch. She made you out to be her knight in furry armor, for chrissake. She's practically begging you to call her."

He really wished that were true. He wanted to call her. He'd picked up the phone so many times Tuesday, he'd actually forgotten he had it in his hand and fell asleep with it that night. But he'd never had the balls to complete the call.

Not even when he'd recalled the look on her face just before he'd left her at her house. She'd been hurt. Not pissed off that he wouldn't sleep with her again. Just…hurt. Like he'd rejected her.

He'd wanted to grab her close and kiss her until neither of them could breathe. Then he wanted to spread her out on a bed and screw her brains out.

They'd connected in the short period of time they'd spent together, shared something special.

"Ah hell."

"Yeah, that about sums it up, cuz." Andy motioned for another beer from the bartender. The German troll, four-feet-nothing and not as ugly as the name would suggest, nodded and drew another draft. "So what are you going to do about it?"

"I have to go to her." He jumped off the stool, barely noticing the wobble in his knees. "I have to tell her—"

Tim's knees gave out on him. Just buckled and dropped him to the floor like a sack of potatoes.

He barely heard the laughter from the other bar patrons and the last thing he remembered seeing was the *Weekly News Journal* fluttering down to cover his face before he passed out.

Friday morning, Carrie stared at her computer screen at the best non-fiction article she might ever write in her life.

All week, she'd cranked out stories for the *Journal* during the day and spent her nights researching. And writing.

After she had all her facts in order, she'd agonized over every word of the article.

Her father would have been proud. Hell, he might've even considered running the piece.

If he ever saw it.

Which he wouldn't.

If the piece was published, Tim would have to leave the area. Hell, he might have to leave the country.

Characters with *way* fewer scruples than she had would crawl all over his property trying to take his picture, get hair samples, maybe even capture him and take him in for tests. Yes, the members of the Society of Paranormal Abnormalities were that nuts.

SPAz was a group of lunatics who believed Jason and Grant from Syfy Channel's *Ghost Hunters* were messiahs. They constantly called the newsroom to provide "tips" or berate the staff for screwing up a story—most of which were half-baked to begin with while the other half were thought up by the staff in alcohol-soaked roundtable discussions, sometimes at the bar down the street.

Who would've believed those idiots actually knew what they were talking about?

But the main reason she didn't want to publish the story remained the same—Tim would leave.

She couldn't believe how badly she'd missed him these past five days. She couldn't imagine how awful she'd feel if she knew she'd never see him again.

Thursday, her car had shown up in the parking lot of her apartment building, towed there by a man who insisted he'd already been paid and told her to have a nice day. She could have sworn she saw two tiny horns peeking out from under his ball cap.

Her car would need a few weeks in the body shop, but she had no doubt it'd be up and running soon enough.

In the meantime, she had a rental. A kick-ass, four-wheel-drive Ford truck that could plow through snow like it was fluffy feathers.

She glanced at the window, noting the time as she did. It was close to nine at night and it was snowing.

She looked down at her feet. Black biker boots, check.

She smiled. Good thing she was always prepared.

* * * * *

Tim hadn't been able to sit still all day.

He tried to keep himself busy, fixing equipment, making lists of supplies he needed to stock for next season, but it'd mostly been an exercise in futility. The TV couldn't hold his interest. Neither could the new J.A. Jance book he'd tried to start several times.

Mostly he paced around the cabin, occasionally stopping by the front window to watch the snow fall. It'd picked up in intensity throughout the day.

He wasn't exactly sure how he'd gotten home from Tioga. He assumed Andy had driven him but after he'd passed out... Well, he didn't remember anything until he'd woken this morning.

He thought about donning his fur and heading out for a ramble through the quiet woods.

But not today.

Damn her.

He wanted Carrie. Wanted her to come back. Wanted her back in his bed so much he got a hard-on just thinking about her. He'd had a hard-on pretty much all freaking week.

And that pissed him off.

Hell, he missed her smart mouth. She'd captivated him in just a few short hours and he wanted more time with her.

Was she working on another article? One that would make her daddy proud?

He wanted to believe she wouldn't do it.

But he hadn't heard from her. And she had to be the one who made the first move. If she'd decided the situation was just too weird for her, that she didn't want to date a guy who could change into a bear... Well, he wasn't going to chase her.

He'd never been ashamed of his heritage. Hell, every family had a few skeletons in the closet, a few eccentrics.

His closet just happened to have eight-foot skeletons and the holy grail for cryptozoologists.

Damn it.

Opening the front door, Tim let the freezing air cool his

frustration. But it did nothing to ease the ache in his chest.

Maybe he'd just give her a call…

The sound of a motor broke through the silence of the snow-covered forest.

His heart began to pound. He wasn't expecting anyone. Andy and Fry had left for points west, promising to call in a few days.

He looked down the lane and saw the steady glow of headlights.

Damn, if he didn't breathe, he was going to pass out. It had to be her.

Idiot. You don't have any idea what she wants.

But he could hope.

It seemed to take forever but finally a pickup truck pulled up to his front door and the woman he couldn't stop thinking about stepped out.

She wore her bright pink coat, her red hair loose around her shoulders, a furious look on her face.

Slamming the door behind her, she stalked over to him, a bunch of white paper in her hand, which she waved in his face.

"You never called."

His eyes opened wide. That wasn't what he'd been expecting to hear and it made what he'd been going to say stick in his throat.

"What the hell are you talking about?" he finally asked. "I didn't know— Wait. Why the hell didn't *you* call?"

"Because I was waiting for you, you big *oaf*."

His mouth dropped open in shock. "What the—"

He didn't get a chance to finish the thought because she threw herself at him, wrapped her arms around his neck and planted her lips on his in a kiss that stole his breath.

He stumbled back a few steps, back into the house, his arms wrapping around her, as much to stop her forward motion as to trap her against him. He wasn't about to let her go for a damn long time, no matter what those papers held.

His lips opened for her tongue to gain access and he groaned as she slipped into his mouth. Her mouth moved over his, almost painful in its intensity. She tasted hot and furious and hungry. For him.

Pushing the door closed with his foot, he set her away from him but only so he could tear at her clothes. He took the papers out of her hand and tossed them across the room. Out of the corner of his eye, he saw them flutter about like Bigfoot-sized snowflakes.

Then he dismissed them and reached for her coat. It'd barely hit the floor when he started working on her pants. But before he could strip the jeans off her, she stepped out of his reach.

Breathing hard, drawing his gaze to the rise and fall of her gorgeous breasts under her long-sleeved t-shirt, she held up one hand in classic stop position.

"I'm still mad at you," she said. But before he could open his mouth to protest, she continued. "I might ruin your clothes. Strip."

It took a few seconds for that to sink in and when it did, he started to laugh.

One of her pale brows lifted but he saw humor flare in those pretty green eyes.

"God, Carrie. I missed you so freaking much."

She smiled. "Me, too. So shut up and get naked."

She started to pull at her clothes and he watched as she bared each inch of sweet flesh while he removed his own clothes. He ripped off his shirt as fast as he could so he only missed a few seconds of her show.

She seemed to be in as much of a hurry as he was because her clothes lay in a pile on the floor before his did. And she had more to take off.

Fully clothed, the woman took his breath away. Naked, she was a goddess to be worshipped. So he dropped to his knees.

Grabbing her around the waist, he lifted her off her feet and laid her out in front of him on the rug. With his hands on her thighs, he spread her wide and put his mouth on her.

He ate at her like he was starving. And he was. A week without her had been hell. He never wanted to be without her again.

Hoped like hell she wasn't here for a quick fuck and then would leave again.

With that thought, he pushed everything else from his head and focused only on making her come.

He sucked her slick lower lips into his mouth for a second before moving his mouth to focus on her clit. He nibbled the tiny bundle of nerves, her throaty moans pumping more hot blood into his cock. Her thighs tried to close around his head but he kept her spread open with his hands on her thighs.

He spent long minutes feasting on her, his hands massaging her thighs as her hands tangled in his hair and tugged, not hard enough to be painful. At least not painful enough to make him stop.

"Tim." Her lust-heavy voice made his cock throb and his balls draw up hard as rocks.

Alternating nibbles on her clit with thrusts of his tongue into her sheath, he worked her, wanting to feel her orgasm. Her hands began to tug on his hair, harder. The pain made him burn hotter, his hands tightening on her thighs.

She moaned his name this time…right before she convulsed as she came.

Her body writhed, her hands releasing his hair to reach for his shoulders.

He drew it out as long as he could but his desire began to claw at him with a life of its own.

With a growl, he crawled up her body, putting his mouth on hers and plunging into her body with one deep thrust.

Sweet Jesus. Heaven.

He tried to go slow but his body wasn't having any of it. His hips hammered into her, his mouth devoured her lips.

She didn't seem to mind. In fact, she urged him on. Her hands reached behind him to grab his ass, kneading the muscles as her legs rose to wrap around his waist.

He was deep but not as deep as he wanted to be.

And he couldn't see her.

He pulled out of her slick sheath, battling her clinging arms and legs. With a quick twist, he reversed their positions, lifting her above him as she reached for his cock to pull it up and impale herself on it.

She started to ride him immediately, planting her hands on his stomach and proceeding to drive him toward his own climax.

The blissful look on her face made every nerve in his body leap with joy. He reached for her hips, just to have that additional connection to her body. Her skin was slick with sweat, sleek and warm.

Their gazes connected and held. She smiled, so sweet he thought his skin might melt.

And he exploded.

* * * * *

"Here, I want you to read this."

Several long minutes after they'd finally caught their breath, Carrie rose, gathered the papers he'd tossed and handed them to him as she sat on the floor in front of the fire.

He took them, though he didn't start to read right away. Just continued to stare at her. Waiting. She knew what he wanted to hear.

"I think it's the best thing I've ever written."

His heart nearly stopped until she continued.

"Kinda sucks it'll never see print," she continued.

His cock throbbed. "Does that mean you're gonna stick around for a while?"

She gave him a little eye roll as her hands moved to her hips. "Does that mean you want me to stick around?"

"Hell, Carrie. I didn't want you to go in the first place."

She smiled as she dropped to her knees in front of him. His cock rose even farther as her breasts jiggled with the motion. "Even though I work for the *Journal*?"

He put his arms around her waist, lifting her off the floor and settling her over his naked lap. "You don't believe any of that stuff's real, anyway. The Loch Ness Monster is a hoax. And there is no Bigfoot."

Her eyebrows lifted in amusement. "And that's just too damn bad, because you know what they say about a guy and the size of his feet..."

THE BIGGER THEY ARE…

STEPHANIE JULIAN

Chapter One

"Are you seriously telling me that network is going to give you hundreds of thousands of dollars to chase after the Abominable Snowman and dinosaurs in Africa? And you signed an actual contract?"

"Yeah, can you believe it? This is my big break, Sis."

Jenna Durham took a moment to consider that maybe the only break had been between her brother's reality and the one everyone else lived in.

Sucking in a deep breath, Jenna made sure she hit the mute button on her cell phone before she blew out a ragged sigh.

She loved her twin dearly. Truly, she did. She'd gone to bat for him every time someone had called him crazy. If she played in the majors, she'd have a .350 batting average.

But Joss had never been what anyone besides his merry band of idiots in the Society of Paranormal Abnormalities would consider normal.

And if Jenna was just the teeniest bit jealous that Joss had the courage—or the foolishly blind determination—to jet all over the world in search of his dream, well, she'd just keep that to herself.

"Jenna?"

She clicked off the mute and forced enthusiasm into her voice. "Joss, that's great. Really wonderful. Where are you going and when do you leave?"

"I've got a flight out in the morning to Scotland. But that's not all I wanted to talk to you about."

Shit. She knew it. He needed money. Joss always needed money.

Hey, Sis, I'm in New Jersey tracking El Chupacabra. *Can I borrow a hundred bucks for raw meat?*

I'm ghost-hunting in Montana. Can you wire me some money for batteries for my EVP?

Hey, Jenna, did you know you can accidentally electrocute yourself by falling into a river with your digital camera strapped to your head with duct tape?

"Joss, I don't—"

"It's not money," he broke in immediately. "Actually this time, I've got a job for you. Just don't say no until you've heard me out, okay?"

Since she'd only just started her fifteen-minute drive from the city of Reading, Pennsylvania, to her adorable little house in the suburbs of Spring Township, she figured what the hell.

Which immediately made her think of that song by Avril Lavigne.

She and ole Avril happened to be the same age, a ripe old twenty-seven. They both had brown hair and a previous predilection for bad boys who liked to skateboard. But that was where the similarities ended these days.

Avril was making a shitload of money while Jenna continued to work as a freelance accountant for small businesses, like Macy Williams, who made cakes in the shape of penises for bridal showers and Doug Millstock, who printed tabloids for such world-renowned groups as the Alternative Christians, People for the Kind Treatment of Llamas and the Association for the Growth of Brilliance.

Last week, Doug had dropped off a stack of "reading material" for her office.

Joss probably already had a subscription to the one on top. The *Weekly News Journal* had a double-issue expose about Bigfoot, complete with pictures.

She had to admit the story had put a smile on her face the entire day. The article had been witty and the pictures just blurry enough to be tantalizing.

She wondered how they'd—

"Wait one freaking minute, Joss." While she'd been thinking, Joss had been talking and her brain had finally caught up. "You want me to do *what*?"

"I want you to go to Tioga County and check out a bar for me. I think Bigfoot hangs out there."

* * * * *

"I don't know what the hell's wrong with me, Fry. It's like I'm sick of sex with hot chicks. I don't even want to pull out my fur coat and terrorize a few backwoods housewives. Dude, I must be dying."

Anadi Lohani, known to everyone but his mother as Andy, knocked back his first shot of Jack and nodded to the bartender for another.

His best friend Fry rolled bright-green eyes and gave his blue-tinged wings a fluttery shake as he laughed. "The only thing you're dying of, my friend, is boredom."

Andy tipped the next shot of Jack down his throat, appreciating the burn and wishing he could actually get drunk. To do that, he'd need another two bottles because his metabolism was so high, it worked alcohol out of his system faster than moo shoo pork through a dog.

"Yeah, so what's the cure, you smartass fae?"

Fry didn't answer right away. Instead, he gave a little wave over his shoulder at the twin sylphs sitting in the booth across from the bar.

Andy followed Fry's gaze and checked out the Irish water nymphs giving him and Fry matching smiles from beautiful mouths as they raised pale, thin hands to return Fry's wave.

The women were gorgeous. Beautiful in the way only Fringe dwellers could be. They had that little something *else* that made them stand out in a crowd.

Even in the crowd here at the Mystyk Bar in Tioga County, Pennsylvania, where everyone was a Fringe dweller.

Hidden in a forgotten valley of the Pennsylvania Grand Canyon and known only to the Fringe, the Mystyk was a safe haven for people like Fry to be able to flap their wings in peace. For the Appalachian Mountain dwarves to cheat the Irish leprechaun out of his gold at their card game in the corner. And for the three Japanese *tengu* at the table by the door to giggle like schoolgirls as they stroked the scales of the Chinese dragon sitting on the floor next to them.

"The cure is sitting right over there at that table." Fry gave the sylphs a devastating smile. "Or would you rather take a shot at the pretty lady in the corner?"

Yeah, the brown-skinned pixie was a beauty but he was afraid he might crush her.

Andy sighed and turned back to his drink. "You know what, Fry? I'm sick of meaningless one-night stands."

Fry froze for a second before he blinked and his dark brows arched in crescents over his eyes. "Whoa, big guy. Now you're starting to worry me. Maybe you better see the doctor. When the hell did you decide to become an adult?"

Andy gave Fry the finger though he didn't bother to deny his friend's accusation. Hell, just yesterday, he'd actually considered having a salad instead of fries with his burger because heart disease would really suck.

Of course, he had the fries because he wasn't that far gone. Yet.

He couldn't say the same for his cousin, Tim. Poor guy had probably bought life insurance and made an appointment to get his balls made into a purse for his girlfriend, Carrie.

"Oh, wait. I know what's going on." Fry's smirk showed off his finely pointed incisors. "This is about Carrie."

Shit, had he said that aloud? Or had Fry just read his mind?

No, Fry couldn't know what he was thinking. He hadn't told anyone about his foolish crush.

Not on Carrie. Well, not *completely* on Carrie. Sure, she was great, a redheaded Amazon built for loving. But Tim had seen her first and Andy didn't poach.

Andy gave Fry his best "you're an idiot" look.

"Oh, don't even." Fry snorted. "You've been moping since we saw them last week."

Fucking Fry. Andy would give his wings a coat of pink glitter if he didn't think Fry would rock the look like every teenage girl's wet dream. Combined with the Scottish accent, the guy had women falling at his feet.

"I haven't been moping, you fucked-up Tinkleberry. I've been thinking."

About how miserably lonely he was and how Tim seemed to have beaten the blahs with the one woman he should've never fallen for.

At least she wasn't a SPAz. The members of the Society of Paranormal Abnormalities were a bunch of idiots who thought they knew all about the Fringe. Turned out they knew only enough to be truly annoying.

No, smartass Carrie Benton worked for a tabloid that liked to print fuzzy pictures of Bigfoot. Just so happened Tim *was* Bigfoot. Cupid definitely had a sense of humor sometimes, the little bastard.

Fry's undignified snort made Andy give his friend a warning glare. Not that Fry ever heeded Andy's warnings. Fry usually brushed Andy off like a fly, which was a damn weird analogy considering Fry had wings and only stood about five-ten, while Andy topped out at seven feet and looked like the Viking offspring of the NBA and the WWE.

The fact that Andy could crush Fry like a bug—pun definitely intended—never entered Fry's mind because he knew Andy would never hurt him.

Hell, violence of any kind was abhorrent to Andy. Why tire yourself out and risk bodily injury beating on someone when you could cut them down to size with a few sarcastic remarks?

Or just terrorize the shit out of them by shifting into his fur coat.

"What?" Andy demanded when Fry just continued to look at him.

Fry rolled his eyes again and lifted his drink for a long swallow. "Dude, do I really have to spell it out for you?"

Well, maybe he did, because Andy wasn't getting Fry's meaning. Which probably had more to do with Fry's attitude than Andy's comprehension skills.

"You're jealous," Fry answered as if Andy had told Fry to go ahead and insult the hell out of him.

Andy drew himself up to his full seven feet, towering over Fry and making the sylphs sigh in unison.

"I am not."

Fry's wings gave a dismissive shake. "Of course you are. Your mom's right, man. We need to find you a woman."

* * * * *

"I cannot believe I allowed him to talk me into this."

Jenna checked the GPS unit again and shook her head when the annoyingly smooth female voice said, "You have arrived at your destination."

"And you're sure this is the place?"

"You have arrived at your destination."

Had her GPS unit just given her attitude? Hell, if a television network—one that had paid real money upfront—had given her brother enough funds to go to Scotland, she figured pigs could fly and GPS units could be snotty bitches.

Considering *she'd* been bitching the entire drive, she wouldn't have been surprised if she'd heard a disgusted sigh issue from the stereo speakers of her new Honda Civic.

But really, what kind of idiot believed in fairies and dragons?

Apparently the kind who got paid actual money to go find them.

Didn't that damn network have better things to do with their money, like make another Saturday night movie as epic as *Megapython vs. Gatoroid*?

Debbie Gibson and Tiffany catfight. A Monkee being eaten by a giant snake.

She'd nearly laughed herself sick.

Or it could have been the fact that she was watching that movie alone on a Saturday night after turning down a friend's request to barhop.

With a sigh, she looked out the front window of the car again.

The next time her brother asked her to investigate some weird bar that catered to monsters in the middle of the freaking Pennsylvania Grand Canyon, she was saying no.

Which would seal her fate as the most boring person in the world.

But really…

Jenna eyed the run-down shack in the middle of nowhere, trying to see beyond the peeling paint and the shuttered windows for any redeeming qualities.

So far, all she saw was a lawsuit waiting to happen when someone put their foot through the rotting floorboards on the porch.

Had someone sent Joss this address as a way to play with his mind?

For the past couple of months, as Joss had gotten more and more convinced that he was close to proving the existence of some of the most incredible creatures in the world, Jenna had considered the fact that maybe someone was leading Joss on. Was there someone out there who had it in for her brother? Who might actually try to lure him out to this remote area and harm him?

Or maybe she'd simply traded Joss' delusions for her own

conspiracy theories.

Jenna stared out at the unrelenting forest, the sight of all that forbidding darkness reminding her of the horror that had been sleep-away camp as a kid.

All those trees. Bugs the size of her hand. And animals that belonged in a nice, safe zoo wandering around without a leash.

What had her parents been thinking when they'd forced her to spend two weeks there?

Hell, she'd always given a wide berth to the neighbor's overly friendly handbag-sized Chihuahua.

Today, camping to Jenna meant a hotel without room service. And she refused to stay in one of those.

This… This was hell.

"I can't believe I let him talk me into this. Jesus, I'm an idiot."

She should just turn around and head back to the lovely bed-and-breakfast about fifteen miles down the road where she'd booked a room for the weekend. It boasted gourmet food, a world-renowned spa and free WiFi.

Civilized.

This place didn't look civilized. It looked almost…prehistoric.

Except for the parking lot beside the shed where six cars sat. Mocking her.

Shit.

Come on, Jenna, you know I wouldn't ask you to do this unless it was important, right?

She and her brother had extremely dissimilar views of the meaning of important.

Joss thought it meant proving there really were prehistoric monsters cruising the Great Lakes. Jenna believed important meant solving childhood hunger and the crisis in the Middle East.

But Joss had pleaded with her, begged and bribed and finally guilted her into promising to check out this place.

Come on, Jenna. If there's nothing there, at least you'll get a weekend away out of the deal and make a couple thousand bucks.

It had been the money that had sealed the deal. She had her eye on a new refrigerator.

"Jeez, maybe you really are the most boring person in the world."

She half expected the GPS to agree. Luckily for its health, it stayed silent. But she knew it was mocking her. She just knew it.

With a sigh, she forced herself to put her car in drive and inch down the lane, which was more like a path, rutted and muddy and suited more for the SUVs and Jeeps she saw in that makeshift lot next to the building her brother thought might hold the Holy Grail of his career.

Career. She snorted. What kind of career could a grown man have chasing myths and legends around the world?

He's getting paid more than double what you made last year, though, isn't he?

Yep. She'd definitely rather fight with the GPS. It was much less snarky than her own brain.

She was happy for her brother. Really, she was. Usually she just nodded and smiled when he talked about the pitiful grants he received from groups like UFOlogists United and The Center for Cryptids and Unexplained Phenomena to "investigate" Bigfoot attacks and poltergeist damage. The UUs and CCUPs of the world were plentiful but they didn't pay very well.

And Joss didn't have a reputable career to fall back on. He was like Indiana Jones without the college gig.

She was the person Indiana Jones would hire to do his taxes.

Damn, she needed to get a hobby. Maybe she'd learn how to skydive. Or maybe she should start with crocheting.

And yes, she was stalling.

The closer she drew to the building, the more her heart started to pound. Instead of pulling into the lot, she parked just shy of it, turning off the car but not removing the key.

She still hadn't talked herself into getting *out* of the car.

She was pretty sure she was trespassing. Even if the sign at the entrance said state park, the sign had also said the park closed at dusk. And that had definitely been a couple of hours ago because right now the only light was that of the moon.

She'd driven for what seemed like forever to get here and she wasn't sure where here exactly was.

Above, the sky shone with *waaay* too many stars. All those tiny pinpricks of light were kind of freaking her out. They looked too damn…cheerful.

Where was a good, old flickering streetlight when you needed one? Hell, she'd feel safer on the streets of Reading at midnight with a homeless guy asking her for money than she felt here.

Here… Mountain lions and bears and wolves, oh my.

Why—

The door to the shack opened, light spilling out into the darkness like a party dress in a dark club. A shadow cut through the light and a man walked out. At least, the shadow was man-shaped.

Her mouth dropped open. Holy crap, the guy was tall. So tall, he had to bend down so he wouldn't hit his head on the doorframe.

Backlit, she couldn't see his face but she did catch a glimpse of blond hair that brushed linebacker-wide shoulders.

The guy stopped to lean against the porch railing, staring up at those same stars, and now she gasped.

In the weak light of the bare bulb over the door, she could just make out his features.

And, oh my goodness, the man was gorgeous. Her heart actually tripped over a few beats on its way back to a normal rhythm.

He didn't look like anyone she'd ever seen before. He looked…a little wild. A little rough. A whole lot gorgeous.

Typically, she dated guys who had their hair styled—their word, not hers—every three weeks and didn't own a pair of jeans that weren't pressed and creased and able to stand on their own.

This guy…

Wow.

The broad planes and sharp angles of his face gave him an exotic, mysterious air. She couldn't decide if he looked Nordic or Asian or eastern European. Probably some combination of all of those and more.

Which just made him absolutely stunning.

And made her tingle from head to toe.

He had blond hair, and she didn't mean run-of-the-mill, department-store gold. She meant Tiffany's platinum. The guy had to spend at last two days a week in a high-end salon to get that shade of white-blond and make it look so damn natural.

And the waves. Tousled waves fell to just below his shoulders, longer than her recently shorn pixie cut.

My God, the man should be hawking shampoo. Or butter substitute. He'd sure as hell sell more than that freaking Fabio.

Then there was that face. His features were such an exotic mix of east and west, broad nose and forehead, sharp cheekbones and eyes that hinted at an Asian ancestry. But his skin tone was definitely on the lighter side of golden.

She'd never seen anyone like him.

And she'd like to see a whole hell of a lot more of him, preferably naked and sprawled on a bed big enough to let them roll around on it. She didn't think he'd fit on the queen-size mattress in her room at the B&B but she'd be more than willing to compromise and let him hog more than his share.

She wondered if *GQ* was holding a top-secret Big & Tall male-model convention in the backwoods of Pennsylvania.

If this guy was one of the models, she was sure as hell signing up for the catalogue. And the calendar and the pay-per-view event.

Please, God, let it be unrated and clothing optional.

As he walked off the porch and started toward her, she knew her mouth was hanging open but she couldn't seem to care.

Not when he wore that quirky grin that let her know he saw her looking at him.

Good old-fashioned lust made her insides turn to liquid even as her nipples hardened into tight points and her thighs clenched like a virgin at a male strip show.

Holy crap.

She knew she'd been suffering from sexual frustration since she'd dumped her last lover five months ago. They'd dated for over a year and she'd never wanted Craig to strip her naked, bend her across the hood of her sensible Honda and make a few dents.

She wished she was the sort of girl to proposition a guy like that. Or any guy she liked, for that matter.

The only propositions she got involved bribes for tax evasion. Not quite enough to make her panties wet.

This guy could probably do it reciting the latest IRS newsletter for CPAs.

Somewhere in the back of her mind was a voice screaming at her to get out of the car, meet him halfway and say, "Hey, you're hot. Can I climb you like a telephone pole and ride you like a cowgirl?"

She wondered if he'd say no. She couldn't imagine the man, who looked like a cross between a Nordic god and the Wild Man of Borneo, hadn't had some pretty far-out come-ons in his time.

What *was* this guy doing out here? For that matter, what was *anyone* doing out here in the middle of nowhere?

What if Joss is actually on to something?

No, that was crazy talk. Crazy talk made you believe ancient aliens built the pyramids.

And no matter how much she admired the skill it took to make Giorgio Tsoukalas' hair defy gravity or the fact that he'd parlayed a totally insane idea into a series on the History Channel, there was no way she believed little green men from outer space had visited Earth to show ancient humans how to cut perfectly square rocks.

Then what is this guy doing here, where there's supposed to be nothing and no one?

She'd done her homework before she'd left home. She'd checked out the coordinates on Google Earth and come up with nothing but trees.

This building stood in a clearing. It should've shown up on Google Earth. And yet it hadn't.

Did that mean someone had gone to great lengths to hide this place? To make it secret?

Or had she finally joined her brother and tasted the Kool-Aid?

No, that was... No.

There was a reasonable explanation for everything. She'd just have to come back in the light of day and find it.

No way in hell was she getting out of her car and asking the hot giant if he could introduce her to Bigfoot.

Chapter Two

Andy had noticed the car parked up the lane as soon as he'd leaned against the porch railing and looked out into the dark forest.

His night vision was good enough to make out the woman in the car. A damn pretty woman who stared at him as if he were an exhibit in a sideshow.

What the hell was she doing here? Who the hell was she? And how the hell had she gotten here?

He didn't recognize her, which didn't mean anything. Except...she smelled totally Normal.

Edible but Normal.

Which meant she really shouldn't be out there staring at the Mystyk Bar as if she'd stumbled onto Shangri-La. Which was absolutely worth staring at for hours.

The outside of the Mystyk...not so much.

Good thing he hadn't shifted to go lumbering through the forest to the cabin he and Fry had rented.

He'd thought maybe he'd get lucky and scare the crap out of a long-haul trucker or two as he made a "classic Bigfoot crossing".

That show *Finding Bigfoot* on Animal Planet had become one of his not-to-be-missed pleasures in life. And that skeptical scientist was kinda hot.

Though not as hot as the girl in the car.

What was she doing here?

Probably better go find out before anyone else walked out of the bar. Didn't want her to get the bright idea that she needed to get out of the car and investigate. Some of the other Mystyk patrons might not be so willing to divert her attention.

They'd mess with her mind for a while then scare the hell out of her until she thought she was crazy.

Of course, maybe he'd found the perfect diversion for his boredom.

Messin' with Normals ranked high on his Most Enjoyable Pastimes list.

Stepping off the porch, he headed toward her car, watching her eyes get bigger with every step he took.

With his hands in the pockets of his oldest, most comfortable jeans and a tight blue t-shirt that matched his eyes, he knew he looked pretty damn good.

Women had been known to swoon at the sight of him.

Of course, just as many had run in the opposite direction, so that pretty much dealt with most of the ego he might've developed.

When he reached the car and leaned down to knock on the window, he decided to start with charm. Save the scare tactics in case the charm failed.

Which he hoped didn't happen because, wow, the lady was a looker.

Her hair was shorter than his, a pretty chocolate brown that perfectly matched those wide eyes and fluttered all around her adorable face. She had soft, rounded features that reminded him of that actress, Reese Witherspoon. Pretty, sweet. The kind of girl you took home to meet Mom.

Not the kind of girl you wanted to strip naked and pin up against a wall.

Which was *exactly* what he wanted to do.

His smile widened and so did her eyes.

"Hey. You okay out here?"

She opened her mouth but he didn't hear anything come out. Her cheeks flushed bright red, showing up as blotches of color on her milk-pale skin.

Her gaze dropped to the steering wheel and she took a deep breath.

Now she could be frightened. A seven-foot guy walks out of a ramshackle building in the middle of nowhere and knocks on your car window. Most people might have cause to fear for their life. Or at least wonder if he hid a chainsaw or meat hook behind his back.

But he didn't think that was what was going on here.

She looked…gobsmacked. In a good way.

In the same way he felt.

He really freaking hoped he wasn't reading her wrong, and he usually had a good sense for these things.

Of course, there had been that one time with that beautiful cat shifter… He'd mistaken a hiss for something other than a warning and… Well, chicks dug scars, right?

He really didn't want this woman to freak out, put the car in gear and scream bloody murder as she drove back to where she'd come from.

So he squatted down until his eyes were level with hers and waited until she turned her head to look at him.

Which she did after a few seconds.

And he was struck again by an urgent need to beat his chest and throw her over his shoulder as he ran to the nearest cave.

Guess he shouldn't give in to that one. Didn't want to feed the stereotype.

He forced a smile back onto his lips, hoping he didn't frighten her anymore.

Looking from his lips to his eyes, she blinked a few times then slowly returned his smile.

And lowered her window.

"Hey," he started again before reining in the urge to say exactly the same thing he already had. "I didn't mean to frighten you. Are you lost?"

Slowly, she nodded, but he couldn't be sure what she was saying yes to—being lost or being afraid.

"I guess I must be. Lost, that is." Her gaze flickered toward the bar for a brief second and he had a momentary thought that she was about to lie to him.

Then she flashed those big brown eyes at him and his brain just keep repeating, *Fire bad, girl pretty*.

He'd have to lay off the *Buffy, the Vampire Slayer* reruns.

"I must've gotten turned around when I got into the park. I was heading back to the bed-and-breakfast and I have such a terrible sense of direction and the GPS didn't seem to be working all that well out here."

Her expression turned apologetic though she didn't bat her eyes as if she were trying to charm a cop into letting her out of a speeding ticket. She looked genuinely guilty and sorry about it.

Like maybe she thought he was a park ranger about to bust her for being in the park after hours.

Damn, wasn't that just the perfect excuse?

And to some degree, you could argue that was true...if you bought the theory that a Yeti shifter had any jurisdiction over a territory held by the Bukwas tribe of shifters, who were based in British Columbia.

Yet, looking into those oh so guilty eyes, he didn't want to lie to her.

What the hell did he say?

"I could show you the way out. I was just getting ready to head back to town. I'll lead you out."

Her gaze shifted back to the bar for a brief second before she smiled up at him. And made his heart thump with a rock 'n' roll beat.

Okay, he definitely needed to spend a little more time with this woman because she was definitely up to something. Something that involved the Mystyk.

Very interesting. If he had a goatee, he'd be stroking it.

He wanted to stroke her instead.

"Let me get my truck and you can follow me back to town."

She smiled at him again and his cock perked all the hell up.

"I'd really appreciate that. Thank you so much."

He thought about sticking his head back in the bar to tell Fry he was going but decided not to press his luck. All those nosy bastards could decide they'd want to get a closer look at the hot chick Andy had found outside.

And that would not be good for so many reasons.

One of which was *not* because he didn't want to share her.

And yeah, that was a total lie.

He got into the Tahoe he kept in his cousin's garage when he wasn't on this continent then drove up to her car. He gave her a stupid little wave and a grin he hoped wasn't too eager then pulled forward so she had enough room to execute a perfect three-point turn in her sensible little sedan.

She didn't crowd him as he wound through several small back roads before he turned onto the main road that lead out of the park and finally to the two-lane country highway back to town.

It took almost a half hour to get back to town, a drive that normally only took fifteen minutes, and that was only if you got behind an eighteen-wheeler doing the speed limit.

Since there was only one bed-and-breakfast in the small town of Bailey Falls, he knew where she was staying.

And, gee, what a coincidence. That's where he was headed too. The cabin he rented was owned by the same couple who ran the bed-and-breakfast.

How convenient was that?

After they'd parked in the lot, he hustled out of the truck so he could open her door for her and watch her slide out of the car.

Damn good call.

Long legs emerged first, encased in formfitting denim that he wanted to pet. Followed by a totally hot set of tits that'd do an all-natural porn star proud. At least a C-cup, if not a D. Damn nice rack.

He wanted to bend down and rub his five o' clock shadow all over them. First he'd pull off that well-worn t-shirt that had some obscure college symbol on it.

Wait, was that...

He started to smile.

Starfleet Academy. Her shirt bore a wickedly artistic symbol that only made sense if you knew what you were looking at.

And since he happened to be a fan, her hotness factor had just gone up about a thousand points.

"Classic or Next Gen?"

Pleased surprise flared in her eyes before she returned his smile. "Classic, of course. And *DS9* had more depth than *Next Gen*, though Picard still rules."

"A woman after my own heart. Kirk was a Neanderthal compared to Picard. The prime directive was more a guideline with James Tiberius than an actual directive."

As they started to walk toward the inn's front door, he realized he'd never gotten her name.

"I'm Andy, by the way."

He stopped at the bottom of the stairs as she climbed to the porch. When she turned to face him, her eyes were almost on level with his.

In the warm, dim glow of the porch light, he saw just how beautiful they were. Golden brown, almost amber.

"Jenna." She held out her hand and he wanted to grab it and lay it on his chest. Preferably while he was naked.

Then he'd move it lower. Slide it down his stomach. Wrap those slim fingers around his dick and show her how he wanted her to touch him.

She must have seen something of what he was thinking on his face, because those beautiful eyes widened again and, when he took her hand, her fingers tightened around his convulsively before releasing him. He didn't want to let her go and had to force himself to do it.

And he definitely wasn't ready to say good night before she took herself off to her bed and he trudged, brokenhearted, to his own. Alone.

"Hey, you wanna get a drink? I know Matt and Birdie have a bar in the lounge for the guests to use. We could," *make out, get naked, have sex*, "talk for a little while."

She blinked. "You know the owners?"

Well, yeah, he did. He'd been renting a cabin from them for years. The mated mountain lion shifters had inherited the property from Matt's parents several years ago.

Frankly, Andy was shocked that they'd rented a room to a Normal, given that their clientele was almost exclusively Fringe.

Now he really wanted to know what this woman was doing here.

He shrugged as if it were no big deal. "Yeah, I've been coming here for years. I like…" roaming the forest and scaring the bejesus out of the occasional hiker "hiking around here."

Her head cocked to the side and he got the impression she was trying to get a read on him. That sharp gaze made him want to fidget like a kid caught passing notes in school.

Of course, if she'd been his teacher…

Then again, he wondered if she had a little plaid skirt and maybe a tight button-down top—

Her lips curved into that smile again, the one he wanted to feel against his mouth. "Sure, I'd love to have a drink."

Yes! He restrained himself from pumping his fist and doing a little victory dance. Since he'd been told he danced like a palsied chicken in its death throes, she'd probably bolt to her room. Alone.

Opening the door, she slipped into the front room of the inn, turning her head to send him a quick, sweetly hot glance over her shoulder. That look would've had any red-blooded man panting after her.

Now it wasn't like women didn't throw themselves at him. They did. Occasionally.

Well, maybe throw was a bad word. Fringe women, at least those who knew him or knew of him...

Some of them actually knew too much about him. They knew he was a nerd who never missed a Comic-Con or an opportunity to dress up as a Klingon. Or Thor.

He even had his own chainmail costume and detailed hammer that been created for him by an Appalachian dwarf long before Marvel had cast an Australian as a Norse god.

Which had actually turned out better than Andy could have hoped. Same with *Iron Man*, though that last movie...

Well, Stan Lee wasn't infallible. Damn near but not totally.

Marvel had had more than a few flops on their hands. The unfortunate *Incredible Hulk* debacle was one. On paper, having Ang Lee direct a superhero movie must've seemed inspired.

But some visions just didn't mix. Some relationships just weren't meant to be.

Daredevil and Karen Page. Nurse Chappel and Spock.

Fringe dwellers and Normals.

Yeah, but look at Tim and Carrie. They're making their relationship work.

Not that Andy was thinking relationship. That was a huge leap from having a drink with Jenna.

Just because they shared a love of *Star Trek* and he wanted to get his hands on the sweet curves covered by those tight jeans and that geeky t-shirt—

Which he loved, by the way.

A woman unafraid to let her geek flag fly. Now that was a woman worth getting to know.

Chapter Three

As she led the way through the charmingly decorated front sitting room to the even more charming den, where the bar was located, Jenna was pretty sure Andy was eyeing her ass.

Which made her self-conscious.

And made her want to let her hips sway just the slightest bit more.

She was a girl, after all, and Andy... Well, Andy made her feel as if she'd swallowed a gallon of Pop Rocks. All tingly and fizzy low in her belly.

He was one big, gorgeous hunk of man flesh. And damn, but he was tall. And perfectly proportioned, not lanky and lean like some guys his height. No, he had broad shoulders and thick biceps and strong thighs. Oh my.

And that hair... A perfectly natural mix of platinum and gold and wheat and honey. She could tell, now that she'd been close to him, that the color didn't come out of a bottle. No one could get that shading that perfectly abstract so that it blended that well.

Jenna had always had perfectly tame dark-brown hair. She'd never really wanted to be a blonde, except for that unfortunate period in middle school. Teenagers could be so cruel. She'd had to live with the nickname Jenna-Ghoul for a year, even after she'd dyed it black for her morose punk phase.

Not that her friends ever teased her. Sure, it'd been tough being one of the only girls in the school who played *Warcraft* and *The Legend of Zelda*. Or even knew that they were computer games.

Most of her friends had been guys with the same love of comic books and role-playing games. Her few girlfriends had explained away her love of *Star Trek* and her crush on an obscure makeup artist named Tom Savini, who created the makeup for George Romero's zombie movies, as a fluke.

Of course, they'd loved her for introducing them to *Harry Potter* nearly six months before anyone in her school had even heard of it. Her mom had bought a book called *Harry Potter and Philosopher's Stone* for Jenna as a gift when she'd gone to a conference in England. She'd forced the book on a few friends, who'd declared her brilliant. For a month anyway. Then she went back to being just Jenna.

She wondered what Andy saw when he looked at her.

An average-looking woman of average height wearing a ridiculous shirt that she loved that her brother had bought for her in Japan on a trip to make contact with the ghosts of Hiroshima.

The bar suddenly loomed ahead of her and she stopped short and turned. Right into Andy's chest. She brought her hands up to brace herself and they landed flat against Andy's abs.

My god, the man was solid as a rock. Her fingers flexed convulsively but his muscles held steady.

And damn, but he smelled good. Like the forest on a crisp, cool fall day. She wanted to rub her face against his chest like a cat. Preferably without the t-shirt in her way. Only her cheek against his warm flesh—

Oh wow. She needed to stop before she had to change her panties. Which might already be too late.

She told herself to take a step back but her feet refused. Or the message got hijacked somewhere between her brain and her feet.

She thought she might have to fight with herself to get her hands to release his chest.

Of course, he wasn't moving away. No, he'd gone statue-still before her. Was he waiting for her to do something?

What would he do if she took another step forward until their toes touched? Would he wrap his arms around her and pick her up until their lips were aligned and her feet couldn't touch the floor?

Her head tilted back and she looked up, and up, into his eyes.

Standing this close, she had a better impression of his size and… Holy Klingon Warrior. Give the man a few ridges on his forehead and a club and he'd win awards at cons across the country.

Then again, give the man a mighty hammer and a cloak and he could pound her—

She blinked and sank her teeth into her bottom lip, hoping to stave off any inadvertent moans she might make, because she now had an image in her head of Andy wearing nothing but a red silk cloak and a grin.

She wasn't thinking Superman. Not clean-cut, wholesome, corn-fed Clark Kent.

No, Andy was much more exotic. His broad features and darker-toned skin and that blond hair contradicted each other every which way but it all worked to make him freaking gorgeous.

For some reason, the *Thundercats* popped into her head. Not that Andy had fur or looked like a cat. No, he was all man.

The exoticness of him reminded her of the crush she'd had on Lion-O, the leader of the *Thundercats*.

Ho! Indeed.

Okay, maybe she and her brother weren't as opposite as she liked to think.

Then again, Joss actually believed the *Thundercats* existed, although he called them werecats and said they lived a solitary life somewhere in India.

"Jenna?"

Wow, that voice. It sneaked beneath her skin and stroked between her legs. It held an accent she couldn't quite put her finger on. She wanted to tell him to just keep saying her name over and over again until she figured it out. Or came just from the sound of it stroking against her skin.

"Yes?"

Andy wished like hell that she was using that word in response to him asking if she wanted to go to his cabin where he would kiss her entire body before settling between her legs and licking her to orgasm.

Right now, he felt every one of her fingers through the thin cotton of his t-shirt, felt those fingers clench into his muscles and watched her gaze drop to stare at her hands.

She blinked then swallowed then bit her bottom lip.

With them standing this close, their size difference hit him. She was at least a foot and a half shorter and the top of her head didn't reach his chin.

He was used to being taller than everyone else. Even in his family, he had at least an inch on everyone.

When he went out, he'd gotten used to the wide eyes and the whispers behind his back. To the pointing.

Yeah, he was a freak of nature. He'd accepted it long ago, embraced it even. Had fun with it.

He'd met women over the years who'd looked at him as if he were an all-you-can-eat buffet and they'd been living on lettuce leaves and water for years. Usually they looked like that was all they'd been eating. Tall, skinny. No tits, no ass.

Not a Victoria's Secret model among them. Usually, they thought he was some basketball player they'd never heard of.

And mostly, he let them think that because otherwise they'd want to know what he did for a living and telling them the truth was out of the question.

Besides, if he told them he was a CPA or some other boring office drone, invariably they'd lose interest. He had a funky sense of humor that not every woman got and the

ones who did... Well, those were the smart ones. The ones who wanted to know what *exactly* he did for a living. What job allowed him to fly around the world seemingly on a whim? Why did he have blond hair when biology would dictate he should have dark?

And why the hell did he have such an obsession for all things odd?

He couldn't tell them the truth. Those smart women would think he was lying and blow him off and the other ones, the not so smart ones... Well, he didn't really want anything to do with them anyway.

Jenna...

The way she looked at him right now... He wanted her to continue to look at him like that. For as long as possible. Hopefully at least until he'd gotten her into bed and showed her just how good a freak could be between the sheets.

Eventually, he'd say something idiotic because, yeah, he was mostly a geek. On top of being a seven-foot Yeti.

But for now, he wanted her to continue to look at him just like this.

After a few more seconds, Jenna drew in a deep breath then slowly withdrew her hands. He fought against the urge to grab her and put them back on his body, preferably lower. And under his clothing.

But he figured he should get to know her better first, possibly even before he tried to get into her pants.

"So," he said, happy his voice hadn't cracked like a teenager's, "how about that drink?"

Her hands dropped to her sides and she tilted her head back, as if he'd startled her. She blinked up at him, her head tilting to the side and her eyes staring so deeply into his, he felt his body straining toward her even as he tried to rein himself in.

Don't do it, you idiot. Don't lean down and kiss her. Don't scare her away.

Finally, she nodded. "Oh, yeah. Sure. Just…um, let me…"

She turned and went behind the bar, bending over to open the fridge.

Damn, he really liked her ass in those jeans.

While she couldn't see him, he reached down to adjust his erection, currently trying to bust through his zipper, before she could come back up and catch him.

"Do you want a beer? Or wine? Or there's soda."

"I'll take a root beer. Matt makes his own. An old Amish recipe he picked up years ago. There should be a few brown, unlabeled bottles in there somewhere."

A half second later, Jenna said, "Aha," and straightened with two brown bottles in her hand and a smile on her lips.

This woman definitely needed to end up in his bed.

He followed her to the overstuffed couch on the other side of the room, where there were more shadows than light. He saw her glance at the table lamp then look away without turning it on.

He hoped that meant she wanted to sit in the dark with him. And all that implied.

Not that she didn't want to be able to see his face.

Damn, man. When did you become such a girl?

Ignoring the inner dialogue that bounced back and forth between, *You're an idiot* and, *Damn, what if she doesn't really like me?*, he took the bottle she held out to him and popped the top. Then he handed that one back to her and opened the other.

His mother would be proud. He wasn't a complete beast. At least, not all the time.

"So what are you doing here, Jenna?"

Her gaze dropped for a second before she smiled up at him. "Oh, just a weekend away. My brother thought I could use a vacation, so he booked me the room. I've never been to this part of the state and I've lived in Pennsylvania my whole life. This area is beautiful."

Now why did he get the feeling she wasn't telling him the entire truth? "Yep, the view's definitely gorgeous."

She blushed and dropped his gaze at his obvious flirting. Sue him. It was second nature and it was totally true. He could sit here all night and stare at her.

"Where are you from, Andy?"

"The accent gave me away, huh?"

Her gaze had strayed to his lips as he spoke and he had to restrain the urge to bend down and kiss her.

Not yet, idiot. You'll scare her away.

"It's really beautiful but I have no idea what it is." She blinked and her gaze shot to his. As if she hadn't been staring at all. "Where are you from originally?"

"Nepal. But we only lived there for a few years when I was a child. Then my family moved around Europe for a few more years." Spreading the legend with them. Good times. "We have relations in the states and I ended up here for high school and college."

Her gaze flew to his hair but he didn't see outright skepticism in her eyes. "Do you get home much?"

"Not as much as I'd like." And he realized that was true. "I miss the mountains. And the snow. But there's also the forests and the temples. It's a different way of life. My parents moved back years ago and I visit when I can."

"Have you climbed Mt. Everest?"

"Yeah, I have." In a way she could never imagine. "So you grew up in Pennsylvania."

Her lips twisted in a rueful smile and her gaze dropped to her root beer for a few seconds. "Yep. Never traveled farther than New York and Florida, though I have been to Las Vegas."

And there was that intriguing blush again.

"Vacation?"

She paused. "Convention."

His lips curved. He knew the reason for that blush. "The *Star Trek* convention."

Her chin kicked up and she looked him straight in the eyes, as if daring him to make fun of her. "Best week of my life. I met William Shatner and Leonard Nimoy."

He settled back into the couch with a full-blown smile. "I met them *and* Patrick Stewart and Marina Sirtis. Always had a thing for Deanna Troi. And Nana Visitor. I think it was the ridges."

Her expression was a revelation. She looked at him as if he'd told her she could wear a red shirt and get a walk-on role in the next film.

God bless J.J. Abrams for ensuring there would be a next film.

Then she started to babble.

About how she'd been a fan since she was eight. How her cousin, a proto-geek who'd been building computers before most people had known they existed outside of top-secret government facilities, had introduced her to the classic series on VHS tapes that he stored in space bags so they weren't overexposed.

How her parents had spent nearly a thousand dollars to buy her the entire series of classic, *Next Gen* and *DS9* when they first came out on disc because she'd wanted them more than she'd wanted a car.

How she'd chosen her senior prom dress because it'd reminded her of one of the dresses in the *Mudd's Women* episode. How she'd loved that they'd finally gotten a female captain in Janeway and how disappointed she'd been when the show had been canceled.

He lost track of the conversation a few times because the sound of her voice mesmerized him.

Good thing he knew his *Trek*, because he was able to weave in and out of the conversation without losing points for not listening. And he was listening.

Really, he was.

Okay, mainly he was watching her mouth. How she'd pause for a few seconds after every couple of sentences, waiting for him to respond, which he would. And then she'd smile when he said the right things, and keep talking.

Which really wasn't a problem except he really wanted to kiss her.

So he was ready the next time. Watching for the pause, he was moving as soon as she started to draw in that breath.

He bent his head and stole a kiss.

Although, he didn't think it was stealing if she didn't seem to mind him taking it.

She didn't freeze, didn't pull away. Her lips remained soft and pliant under his but she didn't return the kiss and he pulled back before he scared her.

As he put more distance between them, he held his breath, watching as her eyes slowly opened and stared up into his.

She looked shocked.

Shit. That wasn't what he'd—

Her arms wrapped around his shoulders and her lips crushed against his.

She kissed him, hard. Her mouth moved against his with an enthusiasm that made him groan and pull her forward.

Her breasts pressed against his chest as he lifted her closer, her legs spreading so her knees settled on either side of his hips. With their height difference, she still had to tilt her head back to keep their lips locked.

His hands molded to her back as her mouth ravaged his. And damn, the woman could kiss. Her lips were warm and mobile and soft against his. He'd never been kissed so well that he was content in the moment to let their lips mingle and mesh.

Usually, he wanted to move on to the *getting naked and getting laid* portion of the evening's festivities. Followed by the inevitable *sorry, gotta go, call ya later* part.

He had the feeling he wasn't going to want to say sorry, gotta go all that soon to this woman. Drawing in a breath, he let the sweet scent of vanilla from her hair and the peach from her skin sink into his lungs. He swore he could taste those flavors on her lips and wanted to feast on her as if she were dessert.

Then she opened her mouth and let her tongue stroke across his lips.

And he swore he saw rainbows flash behind his eyelids.

His groan echoed through the room, probably loudly enough to wake the rest of the guests, though he wasn't sure anyone else had returned from the Mystyk yet.

It wouldn't be long before someone found them, making out like a couple of teenagers.

Although what he wanted to do to this woman went way beyond making out. He had an image in his head of Jenna tied naked to his bed.

For some strange reason, he also had a vision of her in a short-skirted red Starfleet uniform and no panties as she sat on his lap on the deck of the Enterprise NCC-1701.

His cock throbbed behind the zipper of his jeans, and his hands moved up her back until he could sink one into the soft hair at her nape. He let his fingers wind through the short strands until he had a firm grip. He wouldn't hurt her but he had a primal need to hold her tighter.

And she appeared to like it.

Her low moan made every hair on his body stand on end and he strained toward her even as she inched closer.

The height difference forced her head back even farther and he knew that had to be uncomfortable.

Besides, they were sitting in a common room where anyone could walk in.

And knowing the people who stayed here, they'd have no problem sitting down and starting a conversation while he had his tongue down Jenna's throat and his hands up her shirt.

He thought about saying something like, "Hey, Jenna, would you like to take this somewhere more private?" But the words got lost in the wet heat of her kiss.

He didn't want to stop kissing her long enough to speak. He was almost afraid she'd come to her senses, take one look at him and run screaming for her room.

Then again, the way her fingers dug into his shoulders like a mountain climber's spikes heading up Everest, she didn't seem to be thinking about anything but kissing him back.

And what a boost to the morale that was.

She wanted him. All seven feet and two hundred fifty pounds of him.

If he ever got her in bed, missionary position was out.

Of course, he wouldn't be complaining when he was lying on his back watching her ride him.

Probably getting ahead of yourself there, hoss.

But now that the image was there, he couldn't shake it.

He groaned into her mouth, his hands wrapping around her waist as he urged her closer against him.

She didn't need much encouragement. In fact, she shimmied even closer.

And Andy had a brief moment to wonder when the piano might fall on his head before Jenna broke away with a little gasp and opened her eyes to stare into his.

"Wow."

Wow was right. At least, he hoped she was having the same wow moment he was. Like, "Oh wow, that was a totally awesome kiss, let's go upstairs where I will rip off all your clothes and ride you like a Christmas pony".

And not, "Oh wow, I can't believe I just sucked face with a guy who could bench press a car and might possibly be the love child of Andre the Giant and Brad Pitt".

All right, maybe Robert Redford. He'd never been a Pitt fan. Dude had way too many kids and Angelina scared the shit out of him. She had more ink than he did, which wasn't saying much because Andy only had one tattoo on the inside of his wrist because that sucker had *hurt*.

He wanted to ask what that wow meant but he knew he shouldn't open his mouth. Knew he should wait until she said whatever was on her mind, because she definitely had something on her mind.

Keep your mouth shut. Be smart for a change.

Hell, who was he kidding? He *was* the guy who bench-pressed the occasional Cadillac if it happened to be in a parking space he wanted. And he enjoyed scaring the shit out of city folk who moved to the country and made the mistake of thinking there really wasn't anything that went bump in the night.

"Would you like to continue this in my cabin?"

She paused and he swore he saw her brain working. Then she took a deep breath, as if she'd made a momentous decision.

"I would love to continue this in your cabin."

Not waiting for her to change her mind, he stood, making sure he kept her in his arms. Her eyes widened but she wrapped her legs around his waist and tightened her arms around his neck.

"I didn't know there were cabins."

He walked through the house, ducking so he didn't knock his head on the doorjambs until he got to the kitchen. "A few. And they're not that far from the house."

Her mouth curled up at the corners as she looked up into his eyes. He wanted to stop and stare, those eyes were so pretty—

"Shit!"

Pain splintered through his brain as the top of his head hit the ceiling fan light. Jenna hissed in sympathy and her face screwed up in an adorable frown.

"Are you okay?" She lifted her hand to rub her palm over the sore spot on his head. He nearly tripped over his feet as he trembled and he had to force his legs to keep going forward.

She started to shake and he clutched her closer.

"Hey, are *you* okay, Jenna?"

Had he hurt her? What the hell—

She burst out laughing and the sound got inside him and lit that fire even hotter.

"I'm so sorry." She put her hand over her mouth but her eyes shone. "I shouldn't be laughing when you're in pain."

"What pain? You laugh and it disappears."

Her laughter cut off and she blinked up at him. He was pretty sure those eyes were going to be his downfall.

"Wow. That's…wow." Her tongue peeked from between her lips for a brief second. "Please don't take this the wrong way…"

He tensed, sure she was about to tell him to put her down and get lost.

"But I think you should go a little faster."

Faster. Yes. He could do faster.

As Jenna wound her arms around him and rested her head against his shoulder, he made it out the back door and down the path to his cabin without dropping her or tripping over something. He wouldn't have been surprised if he'd actually stepped on his tongue.

Kicking the door closed behind him, he almost expected her to turn shy on him, or at the least, make him continue the seduction.

But he'd barely loosened his hold on her, ready to set her back on her feet, when she tightened her legs and took his mouth in a sinful kiss.

Chapter Four

Jenna let herself drown in the heat of Andy's mouth.

She'd never kissed a guy like this before. With her entire concentration. It made her crave him with an intensity she'd never experienced.

Her hands gripped his broad shoulders before sliding down to his hard biceps. God, the man was built like a... Well, like a god.

Her breasts pressed against the solid wall of his chest. Her legs remained wrapped around his waist, her thighs registering the tight flex of muscles there.

She couldn't wait to get him stripped down so she could run her hands along those tight, powerful muscles.

Her brain had a moment to think, *Are you really going to do this?* Which her body answered with a resounding, *Hell, yeah.*

She was already wet and achy for him. And despite his size, he'd been so careful with her.

If he was going to hurt her, he'd had ample time. But she sensed absolutely no danger from him. And working in the city, she'd acquired a well-developed danger antenna.

Here...now, all she felt was lust.

She slid her hands to his back, bunching his shirt in her fingers and pulling it up. She knew she'd have to release him to get it over his head but her legs weren't getting with the program. They wanted to cling.

Compounding matters, her pelvis rocked forward, rubbing against his stomach, pressing the seam of her jeans into her clit. Yes, right there.

She moaned into his mouth. She wanted his big, blunt fingers right there, pressing the exact same way. Wanted to feel the heat of his skin against hers.

Wanted to see what he looked like naked and spread out on the ocean-sized bed she'd noticed before she'd attacked him.

Okay, maybe attack was a little harsh but that was how she felt.

She wanted to tear off his clothes, fling him on the bed and pounce.

It was almost like a compulsion, as if she'd been put under a spell. But she, the levelheaded sibling in the Durham family, did not believe in magic. This was pure, old-fashioned lust.

Finally, she unclenched her legs and let them straighten. Andy immediately set her on her feet, his hands tightening on her waist before he released her completely.

Now she looked up until she could look into those dark-blue eyes that stared back so intently.

She saw lust held in check, waiting for her signal to be released.

She reached for his belt buckle, figuring he'd get the hint.

He got the hint.

He reached for her shirt, gripped the hem and tugged up. Since she was busy with his belt, he didn't get it very far. And she wasn't about to lift her arms until that buckle surrendered. And it would surrender.

As her fingers fumbled, Andy's grew more sure. He lifted her shirt as far as he could get it then stroked his fingertips along her sides.

She nearly melted from the heat. Then she shivered with desire. Okay, maybe she could give the belt a pass for the moment because Andy had magic fingers.

He played them up and down her sides, raising goose bumps and her body temperature. Each time he moved them up, he got closer to touching her breasts. And each time, he stopped just short.

She wanted— No, she *needed* those huge hands on her. On her naked skin. Which meant he'd have to use those hands to strip her.

"Andy."

"I love your voice."

Oh wow. And she loved his, that dark, husky tone that made her insides quake and made her think of dark, thick chocolate dripped all over that broad chest so she could lick it off.

"Then listen to me and take my clothes off."

That quick grin of his surfaced and she nearly had to cross her legs to make sure she didn't leap at him.

"Lift your arms."

She did what he wanted because she wanted the same thing.

With her arms straight up, Andy grabbed the hem of her shirt and stripped it over her head then unclipped her bra so when she put her arms down, it slid off.

When Andy put his hands on her breasts, the sensation nearly made her come. His fingers plucked at her nipples, sending bolts of pleasure straight to her clit. Her lips parted to take in more air for her oxygen-starved brain but Andy bent his head to seal her mouth with his. The angle was awkward, though, because the man was so tall and he pulled back.

Which gave her the opportunity to get back to that belt buckle. As he yanked his shirt over his head, she finally got the buckle to cooperate so she could unbutton his jeans and—

She actually froze for a brief second to admire the perfect proportions of the man's sex. Not grotesquely huge but large enough for her to say a quick thank-you to Santa Claus for finally answering her wish and bringing her a man with a cock that could give her vibrator a run for its money.

Andy's erection stood proud and strong and stiff enough to hang a flag on it. Or make a girl very happy.

With one hand on his chest, she pushed him back toward the bed until the back of his knees hit the mattress and he went down like a tree. Good thing the bed was huge. And sturdy.

Then he smiled at her and held out his hand. "Come here, Jenna. Climb on."

She didn't need a second invitation. Shedding her shoes, socks, pants and underwear—thank God she'd worn black satin instead of white cotton—she climbed onto the bed then knelt by Andy's side.

So much man. Where should she start?

Apparently at his cock, because her fingers had already wrapped around the iron-hard shaft and begun a slow, sensuous glide. Up. Down. His skin, silky soft, warmed against her fingers. The underside was particularly soft and she let her fingers play over that spot again. A smile curved her lips when Andy groaned and his eyes rolled back in his head.

"Jenna."

She loved hearing him say her name. Loved knowing she was the one who made his hands clench into fists in the bed quilt.

Tightening her hand around him—and sighing when she realized her fingers didn't meet—Jenna slipped her other hand between his legs to cup his heavy balls.

He hissed in a breath and her hands froze as her gaze flashed to his face. Had she hurt him—

"Jenna, Jesus, don't stop."

The impassioned plea in his voice sent a shiver through her, making her nipples harden into throbbing points and her sex clench, almost painful in its intensity.

She'd never wanted anyone as much as she wanted Andy and knowing she was going to have him made her want to put off the actual act just a little while longer.

Sweet, sweet torture. Andy's wide chest rose and fell in a ragged rhythm and she leaned forward until she could nip at one flat nipple.

"Ah, shit."

Andy shuddered as she did the same to the other then bit her way down his chest to his stomach until her lips were millimeters away from the firm, wide head of his cock.

She swore his breath stopped as she pressed a kiss to the tip in preparation for taking him inside. But Andy rolled to the side and she had a second's doubt before he reached into the bedside table and came back with a condom, which he held out to her.

Torn for a brief moment between not wanting to let him go and getting to the really good stuff, she grabbed the condom and sheathed him, making sure to tease him as she rolled it on.

When she had him covered, she sat back to survey the manscape, her smile growing wider by the second.

She contemplated slinging her leg over his hips and just riding him like a cowgirl. He must have read her mind, because he grabbed her around the waist and lifted her right where she wanted to be.

Which was spread over his hips.

Her lungs felt starved for air as Andy pulled her down while she pulled his cock back, handling him with as much care as he held her.

She thought about teasing him some more but decided she didn't want to wait. She needed to sink down onto all that firm flesh, take it in then ride him until they both came.

With her gaze on his, she lowered her hips until the tip met her sex. Already wet, she slicked the broad head of his cock with her juices, teasing them both with the heady sensation. Shivers ran through her, causing her sheath to tighten and pulse, already so close to climax, she was almost embarrassed.

But the way Andy stared at her, the way his gaze was glued to hers instead of her body, watching her reactions, obliterated everything but the desire.

Slowly, she sank, hissing a little as he stretched her, silently praising his girth because god knew she didn't want to say anything stupid aloud but, damn, he felt amazing.

She sank until they were fully joined, her eyes nearly rolling back in her head. They sat there, the only sound their heavy breathing.

Then Andy shifted his hips and tiny fireworks began to pop and sizzle in her lower body. With his strong arms, he lifted her as his hips withdrew, his cock sliding from her until only the tip remained. Then he let gravity do its thing and Jenna decided she was going to worship Isaac Newton, just as soon as she could think again.

Andy started to increase the pace, the muscles in his arms bunching and releasing, providing a stimulating visual that engaged her brain and her body in the act.

It was his expression, though, that made her nearly incoherent with lust. He looked just as lost as she felt. His eyes glazed and barely open, his lips parted. Each finger a brand on her skin.

Sensation built until she felt like a bottle of soda, corked and shaken until she couldn't contain the pressure any longer. She tried to hold on, tried to retain that edge but...

She exploded, her hands reaching for his wrists as he let her sink until he was buried deep inside, pulsing through his own release.

And when she couldn't hold herself up anymore, he drew her down onto his chest.

Wow. That was... Wow.

Chapter Five

I really should get out of here.

Jenna stared at the wall of the Andy's cabin, intensely aware of the heavy arm he had around her waist.

Heavy, but not unwelcome.

Actually, she really liked it.

She liked how big he was. How she felt so completely surrounded by him when they curled together like this. The man gave off enough heat to keep her warm if they were stranded on the ice planet of Hoth. She liked that too.

So why, exactly, should she leave?

She'd had the best sex of her life last night. With a man she'd met only minutes before she'd torn off his clothes.

She should be embarrassed. She didn't do things like this.

But, oh my. It had been amazing.

Or...maybe she'd just been depriving herself and last night hadn't been as good as she'd thought.

She sighed. No, that definitely wasn't it.

So why did she have the overwhelming urge to leave before he woke?

Behind her, Andy shifted and all that naked skin rubbed against hers and she swore she was going to melt.

The arm currently cushioning her head moved lower until he wrapped it around her shoulders, drawing her even closer. She wriggled against him until she felt the wiry hair on his legs brush against the skin of her butt, forcing her to stifle a lusty sigh.

Which became that much harder to do when the arm around her waist tightened and one huge hand engulfed her breast.

Heat shot through her as her head angled back. Behind her, Andy nuzzled her before he opened his mouth and bit the tender part of her neck where it joined her shoulder.

Geez, this was better than an alarm clock any day. And that firm, hot cock pressing against her butt cheek… She wanted to spread her legs and take him inside.

What happened to leaving?

No way was she leaving now, not when things were just getting interesting.

"Good morning."

His words rumbled through his chest and vibrated against her back, making her shiver with anticipation.

"Good morning."

"How did you sleep?"

Considering how little sleep she'd gotten, she was amazed at how great she felt. Usually if she didn't get at least six hours, she felt like roadkill.

Not this morning.

She felt…vivid. Alive. Horny.

Amazingly horny.

Who knew it would take a seven-foot blond god to light up her libido?

About to roll over and see just how much better she could feel this morning, she stopped when she heard the unmistakable ring of her cell phone. She knew it had to be hers because she didn't think Andy had the theme from *Farscape* as one of his ringtones.

Having a brother who knew his way around a computer editing program did occasionally come in handy.

Except that was Joss' specific ringtone.

"Do you have to get that?" Andy pressed closer, making it clear he would be more than happy to take her mind off whatever Joss wanted. She stifled a groan. What could Joss possible want this early—

Wait, it wasn't this early in Scotland. It was actually probably midafternoon. Maybe something had happened? What if the money had fallen through and he was stranded somewhere in Great Britain? What if—

"Jenna, are you okay?"

Damn it, she really wished she could say yes to that and mean it.

"Yes, I'm fine. I just need to answer that."

With a sigh, she slid away from Andy, from the heat of his body and the temptation of all that naked flesh.

Which of course meant he could see her in all her naked glory. She didn't have many hang-ups about her physical appearance. She kept in shape and if she had a few more pounds than she wanted, at least she carried them in her breasts and ass. Both of which Andy didn't seem to have a problem with.

Still, she reached for Andy's shirt on the floor and pulled it over her head even as she reached her pants and grabbed the phone from the pocket. "Hey, Joss, what's up? Is everything okay?"

"Jenna, where are you?"

She frowned. Her brother sounded worried. Joss never worried. Not when he was lost in some state park in Maine in the middle of winter and definitely never about her. He knew she was steady as a rock.

Except, the proof of the decaying bedrock of her stable life was still in the bed they'd nearly destroyed last night.

"Um, I'm at that little B&B in Tioga we talked about. Remember, we discussed this trip before you left."

She didn't want to say too much because she didn't want Andy to overhear anything. Especially not anything that might make her sound as if she was chasing crackpot cryptids, like her brother.

"You actually went? Damn, Jenna, for the first time I was hoping you'd ignored me. Doesn't matter. You gotta get out of there. And fast."

A shiver ran up her back at Joss' anxious tone. "What are you talking about? You're not making any sense. First you tell me I have to do…something for you and now—"

"Now I'm telling you to go home. Right now. I don't have time to go into everything, but you need to get out of that town. Now."

"Joss, slow down—"

"I can't. We're getting ready to board the plane and we're going to get cut off. And they're confiscating our cells."

"I thought you'd already left for Loch Ness?"

"Change in plans. Look, Jenna, if you trust me at all, please just go home. There's nothing there. I was totally wrong. Just go."

Now he was really starting to freak her out. "Are you okay, Joss?

Did you hit your head or something? Do you have a fever, nausea? Did something bite you? Did you eat something you shouldn't have?"

She wouldn't put it past Joss to have tried some mushroom because the locals told him it would help him see the monsters better. Or to have been bitten by some wild animal as he trekked through remote forest.

"Jenna, this isn't about me. I'm fine. You just need to leave—"

The connection clicked off in her ear and she lowered the phone to stare at the blank screen.

What the hell?

"Jenna? Are you okay?"

Andy's voice sounded strained but she put that down to her own baffled confusion.

Hell, five minutes ago, she'd been thinking about doubling the amount of great sex she'd had in her life. Now...

"Jenna?"

"Yes?"

She turned to find Andy staring at her with an expression she couldn't decipher. Almost as if he looked sick to his stomach.

"I'm sorry." She shook her head. "My brother..." She sighed. "He's worried about me for some reason."

"And your brother is...?"

She frowned before she could stop herself. Why did that sound like an odd question? Almost as if he wanted her to spill secrets.

Maybe she was reading too much into Andy's tone, but...

He almost sounded like he knew who her brother was. Which was crazy, right? She hadn't told Andy her last name, which seemed kind of silly now, considering he knew exactly how she liked him to stroke her clit to make her come.

So she deliberately misunderstood his question.

With a weak smile, she said, "Not usually a worry wart. He's a..." Crackpot who believes in Bigfoot and the Jersey Devil. "He's on a business trip to Scotland. I don't have any idea what would set him off like this."

Andy had no idea what would have set off Jenna's brother.

Then again, he'd had no idea Jenna was Joss "That *fucking* SPAZ" Durham's sister before he'd slept with her.

Holy shit. What the hell were the odds?

Too fucking high.

So she can't be.

Yeah, she is.

No way.

Yes—

Christ, he felt like Gollum. And that was not only creepy but depressing.

Joss Durham was the king jester of the idiot brigade otherwise known as the Society of Paranormal Abnormalities, a group dedicated to proving the existence of what they called cryptids.

SPAz was what the Fringe society called the self-proclaimed "researchers"—and yes, he used that word loosely—who believed in Bigfoot and the Loch Ness Monster and *El Chupacabra* and a whole lot of other things that other people knew were fictional.

Only they weren't.

And the SPAz... They weren't dangerous so much as a major pain in the ass. Most Normals wrote them off as crackpots, which was just what the Fringe dwellers wanted.

But some of them, like Joss, were a little smarter than the average bear. And when they got an idea in their head, they were like starving terriers with a bone.

Most Fringe dwellers gave the SPAz a wide berth, but some took the time to screw with their heads for fun. Hell, he'd messed with Joss personally a few times. The guy had an uncanny knack for showing up at the right place at the wrong time.

Like when a seven-foot, shape-shifting Yeti was visiting his American Bigfoot cousin and they decided to take a run through the woods to work off some steam.

That episode had been more than two years ago, and the couple of fuzzy pictures Joss had gotten had only made it as far as a few cryptid blogs.

Still, the guy was tenacious and surprisingly smart for a SPAz.

"So, your brother...what does he do for a living?"

Her expression turned even more pained. It was obvious she didn't want to talk about Joss. Hell, she was downright embarrassed.

She didn't believe, not like her brother.

And now he didn't know whether to be relieved or bummed. What would she do if he flipped the switch and pulled on his Yeti form right now?

With another woman, he might have gotten a laugh out of it. At the very least, a chuckle.

So why did he feel like a teenager who'd just been told Justin Beiber had married Lil Wayne and they planned to adopt a couple of kids and move to Europe?

Jenna dropped her gaze to her hands, twisting in knots in front of her. "He just got a new job, as a matter of fact. Filming documentaries."

Shit, shit, shit. "Oh yeah?" He tried to force some enthusiasm into his voice but it was like trying to smile while eating dirt sandwiches. "What kind of documentaries?"

Whatever she heard in his voice made her entire demeanor change. She stopped fidgeting, her hands went to her hips and she lifted her chin in the air as if she were going to battle City Hall for the right to sell lemonade on a street corner.

"The first one is about the Loch Ness Monster. After that he's heading to France to do one on *loup garou.*"

Yep. No doubt about it. She was Joss' sister.

He'd had the best sex of his life with the sister of his sworn enemy. Now he'd have to battle Joss with lightsabers on an inner-planetary playground—

Dude, overreact much?

He wanted to roll his eyes at himself. This wasn't *West Side Story*, for chrissake. This was more like the soft-core History Channel version.

A Yeti and Joss Durham's sister walk into a bar...

There was no way that joke ended with anything other than a bad punch line.

But damn, Jenna Durham sure packed one hell of a punch.

Andy thought she was absolutely beautiful. Especially with her hair mussed from sleep, wearing his shirt with her chin stuck in the air, daring him to say something asinine about the brother she obviously loved, even though she thought Joss was just a little off his rocker.

He should do it, piss her off so she stomped off in a huff.

And he would never see her again.

"That sounds…interesting."

He offered her a lopsided smile because he couldn't treat her like some backwoods nutcase who told people like Joss about their midnight encounter with Bigfoot. Sure, some of them happened to be telling the truth but still…

As she took a breath, Jenna's shoulders softened and so did the look on her face. Her mouth curved back into a gentle smile and damn, if his cock didn't sit up and make him want to beg her to come back to bed.

"Thank you. But I know how it sounds. It sounds crazy. But Joss isn't crazy. I mean, not really. He's just…passionate." Her smile had brightened as she started to believe her own story but now started to fade again. "Honestly, I don't think he's ever going to find any definitive proof. I mean, who really believes those stories about dinosaurs in the jungle and blood-sucking creatures in the New Jersey badlands?"

She stared into his eyes, as if pleading with him not to look too unkindly on her brother. She'd probably gotten more than her share of condescension from people who knew Joss and lumped her into the same fanatical group.

Only Joss wasn't crazy.

There really were blood-sucking creatures in New Jersey except they didn't live in the badlands. They lived in Trenton, which could conceivably be considered the worse of the two locations. At least the *chupas* thought so.

Dinosaurs? Well, he figured you couldn't blame the Normals for mistaking dragons for prehistoric lizards. They did have common ancestors, after all.

Jesus, how the hell did he get himself into these situations?

Fry was probably laughing his ass off at the moment, although he wouldn't know why. He'd always said some day karma was going to bite Andy on the ass.

Guess he'd be picking teeth out of it for a while.

"What about you, Jenna? What do you believe?"

What did she believe?

Now that was a loaded question, wasn't it?

Jenna knew what her answer should be. She should smile, laugh a little, maybe shake her head and say of course she didn't believe in Bigfoot. What person in their right mind would?

But her brother wasn't crazy. Just a little…misguided.

"I believe there are probably creatures in the world we haven't discovered yet."

It was her stock answer when defending Joss. She'd perfected it over the years, gotten it down to as few words as possible so there was less to argue or discuss. And she hoped Andy would let the conversation die a natural death.

She'd really rather be doing something other than talking.

Because sex like they'd had last night was just as elusive as finding a living dodo bird.

"So what do you do for a living, Jenna?"

Annnnd now she was going to bore him to tears and he'd be hustling her out the door and back to the bed-and-breakfast with an "I'll call you" and a pat on the ass.

Then again, maybe she could distract him with sex.

Jenna never really thought of herself as a sexy person. She had all the necessary parts but when she thought about being deliberately sexy…well, she ended up more as a cross between Zooey Deschanel in *The New Girl* and Mayim Bialek on the *Big Bang Theory*—a cute dork who occasionally walked into closed doors because she was too busy thinking about tax deductions and getting excited about finding an extra thousand dollars in refund money for the *bodega* owner down the street from her office.

But she was still a dork. And while that might work for some guys, that wasn't how she wanted Andy to remember her.

Instead of answering, and before she could have second thoughts, she stripped the t-shirt over her head, dropped it on the ground and gave him her best attempt at a sexy come-hither stare.

Which she didn't think he noticed, because his gaze immediately dropped to her body.

Her chest, to be more precise. Andy was definitely a chest man. His gaze stayed glued to her breasts as she walked over to the bed, careful not to trip over the various pieces of clothing littering the floor. She didn't think Andy would've noticed if she had. His gaze was fixated on her naked body.

Which she had to admit was pretty freaking arousing. It'd been dark the first time. She hadn't caught more than a few glimpses of the full glory of Andy's nudity. And she had to admit she wanted to turn on all the lights, open all the windows and let the light pour down on all that gorgeous man flesh. All seven feet of him.

As a matter of fact...

She stopped at the side of the bed and reached for the sheet covering his lower body. He barely noticed as she pulled it away from him, baring him completely.

Her mouth actually watered, that's how gorgeous she found him. Tight muscles. Long, lean limbs. Huge, hard... Oh yeah.

She reached for that huge, hard shaft, already stiff and straining upward. So soft, so male. So irresistible.

She wished she had the courage to bend over and take him in her mouth but...

Well, why the hell not? This was her fling, after all. She was never going to see Andy again. And even if that thought gave her a curiously hollow feeling in her stomach, it also gave her more of a sense of urgency. And a sense of freedom.

Without releasing him, she knelt on the mattress beside him, gently grasped his cock then bent until her lips touched the thick crest.

She thought she heard Andy gasp but it sounded kind of garbled. Like maybe he'd almost swallowed his tongue.

She liked the idea that she'd surprised him. She also liked how he got even harder as she wrapped her hands around the shaft and let her lips and tongue play over the head.

"Damn, Jenna..."

He sounded breathless but the hand he laid on her head didn't force her down. Instead, he cupped his hand on the back of her neck then let it slide down her spine before he dipped around to her front to cup her breast.

Even as he began to pant like a freight train, his cock straining, his fingers didn't pinch too hard. Just hard enough. Her nipples felt tight, almost painful to the touch.

If she could've panted she would have. As it was, she was much too intent on making him come with her mouth.

He'd become her favorite treat and she loved the way he tasted.

So when he groaned and lifted her away from him, she actually thought of resisting. For all of about two seconds because she realized then that she wanted him to fill her.

Before she realized what he was up to, he'd set her on her knees and crowded behind her. His fingers stroked against her sex lips, slid over her clit, teasing her.

Slippery now with her moisture, his fingers glided inside her, only just penetrating. Not enough to really fulfill her.

She wriggled against him, trying to get him to sink deeper, but he used his free hand to tap her ass. It didn't sting, but it did tingle enough to make her wonder if she'd like him to smack her a little harder.

So she wriggled again but this time he did go deeper.

As she moaned his name, her sex gripped his fingers tight, trying to suck him in.

Instead he withdrew.

She barely had time to breathe out a denial before he slid back in, this time to the base of his fingers.

And when he twisted them inside and stroked, she felt a quick, sharp orgasm cut through her.

Not enough. Never enough.

"Not yet, babe," Andy growled out. "Hang tight."

Withdrawing, he reached for a condom from the drawer. Seconds later, his cock nudged at her entrance then he thrust inside and rode her. No time for slow. This time it was fast and hard.

And she loved every thrust and retreat. She loved the way he'd push inside, his hands tightening around her hips as if he wanted to drag her as close as he could get her.

"Jenna, are you close?"

"Yes, just...oh yeah, right there."

Jenna moaned as he hit that spot that made her melt, made her body shudder and her orgasm spread like a starburst.

Arching her back, she tightened around him, heard him gasp out her name then felt the pulse of his cock inside her.

As she deflated onto the bed, Andy came down beside her, careful not to put too much of his weight on her.

Damn, she could get used to this.

Too bad she had to leave. And never see him again.

Chapter Six

"So, I really should be going."

Andy had been dreading this part.

They'd gotten dressed but had only made is far as the couch before he stole one last kiss, which had turned into fifteen minutes of necking.

He couldn't seem to get enough of her but it was close to noon and she'd said she had a long drive.

Damn it, he did *not* want Jenna to go even though he was pretty sure he shouldn't want her to stay.

She had to be here investigating a rumor for her brother and she'd been too close to the Mystyk Bar last night for it to be coincidence. The fact that he'd never heard of Joss having a sister until now probably only meant he'd been keeping her as a stealth weapon.

It'd be too much to hope that her being here was mere coincidence.

"Do you have somewhere you need to be?"

A blush turned her cheeks rosy and Andy felt his stomach twist.

"Actually, this is going to sound really stupid. And now that I'm here, I know how foolish it really is, but... No, never mind. I have to get home. I've got work that needs to be finished and...stuff I need to do. I really would love to stay but..." again that blush, "I really should get back to real life."

Real life, huh? So what had last night been?

"I had a great time last night, Andy."

She smiled at him and all the heated anger that'd started to gather in his chest at being considered something less than real sank lower. Really low. And definitely was no longer angry.

Hell, he'd finally met a girl who turned him on like no one he'd ever met but he should be glad she was going.

This situation totally sucked.

But what the hell could he do about it?

"I had a great night too. Can I at least get your number? If I ever get back through," he remembered at the last second that she'd never actually told him where she lived, "here, maybe I could give you a call?"

Her cute little nose wrinkled. "Actually, I'm not from around here. I live closer to Reading, which is about an hour north of Philadelphia. But if you ever get down there…"

Well, hell, wasn't that almost too convenient. His cousin Tim didn't live far from Reading.

Maybe Tim would get a few more visits a year than he was used to. Carrie wouldn't mind. She could always use some pictures of a Yeti for her magazine.

"I'm sure I could manage it."

Her undiluted smile made him want to throw her back on the bed, strip off the clothes she'd just put on and get her to agree to stay for the rest of the day, at least. Maybe the next day, as well.

But what he really should be doing was pushing her out the door and on her way home. Away from here. Away from him and his Fringe friends.

If Fry found out who she was, he'd never hear the end of it.

Come to think of it, he hadn't heard from Fry at all last night. No texts, no calls asking where he'd gotten to. Maybe his buddy had gotten lucky too. Probably not as lucky as Andy but maybe he'd picked up a woman at the bar and went back to her room. The guy was as chick magnet. Something about those wings…

Then again, what if something had happened to him?

Nah, someone would've called him. If Fry had gotten drunk—and that was a damn good possibility—he wouldn't have been able to fly so there would be no smashed Fry on a tree or a windshield somewhere.

Someone had probably given him a drive back to the B&B where he was sleeping it off in a room.

"Andy, is something wrong?"

He blinked and realized Jenna's smile was gone. Probably because he'd started to frown.

"No. Nothing's wrong. I just realized I didn't tell my friend where I was going last night and I haven't heard from him since then."

"Do you think something happened to him?"

"No... No, I'm sure he's fine."

"Maybe you should give him a call. It'll make you feel better. And I really should check in with my brother again."

And there was the invisible pink elephant in the room again.

"I had a great time last night, Jenna. And I really do want to see you again."

Damn, her smile made him horny as all hell.

Turning, she began to look around the room then turned toward the desk. She jotted down something on the notepad by the phone then headed for the door.

She opened it but turned back to him before walking out. "I'd really like to see you again too. I left you my number. Plea—"

Jenna disappeared with a squeak.

For a second, Andy blinked at the space where she'd been standing. In the next, he ran for the door, his body obeying signals from his subconscious before his sex-addled brain realized what had actually happened.

Throwing open the door, he stepped outside and assessed the situation. Then he took two strides and grabbed the guy trying to drag Jenna down the path toward the B&B. The guy couldn't have weighed more than a hundred pounds soaking wet and barely came up to Jenna's shoulder. Andy would've thought it was a kid except for the scraggly beard covering his chin and the receding hairline.

The guy squealed and released Jenna when Andy picked him up by the scruff of his neck and let his feet dangle inches above the ground.

Jenna turned, hands on her hips, a furious expression on her face. "Mike, what the hell's going on with you? What're you doing here? And why the frack are you trying to kidnap me?"

The tone of Jenna's voice made it clear she knew the guy. And wasn't happy to see him.

The look on the guy's face was sheer panic. Andy was surprised ole Mikey here wasn't begging for his release.

"Joss wanted me to make sure you were okay. He didn't want

anything to happen to you."

Jenna's arms crossed under her breasts now and Andy couldn't help but sigh at the sight. "And why exactly would he think something would happen to me?"

Mike flicked a somewhat frantic look at Andy over his shoulder as his feet pedaled in the air. As if he might be able to get enough motion going to get free. Andy just lifted his eyebrows at the SPAz. Definitely SPAz.

His new buddy Mike had that look about him.

"Joss just wanted to be sure you got his message. Since I was in the area, I told him I'd make sure you were okay."

"Bullshit."

Andy's mouth quirked in a grin at the heat in Jenna's tone. He really liked this girl. And when she caught his grin and returned it, that heat sank into his blood.

"I want to know what's going on and I want to know now. Andy, I think you can let him down. He may be an idiot but he's not dangerous."

Andy would reserve judgment on that one. Not on the idiot comment. That was definitely true.

As soon as he put the guy on the ground, Mike made a beeline for Jenna, and, while he didn't exactly cower behind her, he did stick pretty close to her side.

Mike must've seen Andy's displeasure with his proximity to Jenna but, even though the guy practically quivered like a hairless Chihuahua in a snow storm, he didn't move.

"Jenna, who is this guy?"

"And why would you think this was any of your business, Mike? What are you doing here? I thought you went with Joss."

Mike flushed a bright, uncomfortable red. "I was going to but my mom needed me at home. She'd be all alone if I left and..."

Jenna actually looked sorry for the guy and Andy had to admit it was kind of pitiful.

"So now you're following me around?"

"No! Well, not really." Mike gave Andy a furtive look before leaning closer to Jenna. "Joss told me why he asked you to come here and I think I found something you need to see."

Well, shit. That didn't sound good but Jenna just rolled her eyes.

"Whatever it is you think you found, Mike, I'm sure it won't interest me."

Mike deliberately ignored her or, more likely, he didn't pick up on Jenna's tone, which definitely told Mike to get lost. Instead, he started tugging Jenna toward the B&B.

Andy was about to go rescue his damsel but the damsel didn't appear to need any help as she made a short, sharp motion and freed herself from Mike's grip. Before he could attach himself to her arm again, and before Andy could grab the guy by the scruff and give him a shake for daring to touch Jenna, she held up one index finger and stared Mike down as if he were a first-grader having a temper tantrum.

If Andy had had a teacher like Jenna, he probably would've flunked out of school because all he'd do all day was stare at her.

Finally, Mike actually stomped his foot like a child. "Jenna, you gotta come with me. Joss will have my head on a platter if anything happens to you."

"And again, I say, I'm old enough to take care of myself. And older than you by five years."

Andy made a mental note not to get on this woman's bad side. That tongue could cut like a knife. When it wasn't licking up his—

"Jesus, Jenna," Mikey's voice had dropped to a level he probably thought Andy couldn't hear. Too bad for Mike, Andy had great hearing. "I've got a freakin' fairy trapped in my trunk. You gotta come see."

It was Andy's turn to roll his eyes.

Well, hell. That probably explained the mystery of what'd happened to Fry last night.

How the fuck did the guy get himself into these situations? This wasn't the first time Andy would have to pull his ass out of the fire. Or, in this case, Mikey's trunk.

But how did he do it without Jenna seeing Fry?

Or maybe…it'd be a good way to gauge Jenna's reaction to the Fringe. Of course, if she turned out to be just like her brother, he'd never be able to see her again. And if she told anyone she'd slept with a Yeti, well, she'd lose any credibility she'd ever had.

Which would be a shitty thing to do to the woman he had a

freaking hard-on for right now.

So what the fuck did he do? He couldn't leave Fry in the back of the little twerp's car, though it would serve Fry right if he did, at least for a little while.

"Now, Mike, really. I know you probably think you have a fairy in your trunk but maybe it's simply a bat or a—"

"Bat's aren't almost six feet tall with blue wings."

Yep, definitely Fry.

"Oh my god." Jenna's expression made Andy wince and Mike practically folded in on himself. "Do you mean to tell me you have an actual person trapped in the trunk of your car?"

"He's not a person, he's a fairy."

"Oh, for—Mike! You're going to get arrested for a hate crime!"

Andy couldn't help himself. He started to laugh even as Mike began to wave his hands in the air as if he were guiding a fighter jet onto the deck of a battleship.

"No, I mean he really is a fairy. He's got wings and everything."

Now Jenna threw her hands in the air and started stomping back toward the B&B. Like a good little boy, Mike fell in behind her. Andy followed at enough of a distance that he could ogle her ass. He figured it'd be the last time he got to see it.

They reached Mike's car in what seemed like seconds and Andy started to laugh again. He couldn't help it.

Mike drove a Gremlin.

The damn thing didn't have a trunk. It had a see-through hatch. The only reason no one had noticed Fry in the back was because Fry had curled in on himself. He looked like a pile of clothes, his dark hair blending into the dark fabric of his coat.

While he tried to hold back his laughter, Jenna and Mike gave him funny looks. Jenna's confusion scrunched up her face in adorable bemusement while Mike just looked pissy.

Just wait, little man. I'll show you something that'll wipe that pissy look off your face in a heartbeat.

"Mike, open this car right now."

"But Jenna—"

"Don't 'but Jenna' me." She held up her index finger and Mike looked like a puppy she'd just taken the newspaper to. "Open. The.

Car."

With a huge sigh, Mike trudged over to the car, pulled keys out of his pocket and fumbled around until he got the right key in the slot.

The hatch popped open.

Fry didn't move and a quick blast of fear swept through Andy that his friend was actually hurt. Then he caught a whiff of alcohol.

Not hurt. Drunk.

How the hell much did Fry drink last night? Not that it took much to knock the guy out. Alcohol did funky things to the fae.

"My god, Mike, did you hurt him?"

"No! Of course I didn't." Mike actually looked affronted that she'd even think that. "But I let him have the bottle of moonshine I had in the car. You remember that trip your brother and I took to Kentucky a few months ago? To track down that Bigfoot sighting? Well, we kinda got lost and stumbled onto this illegal moonshine ring. They held us hostage for a few hours before they realized we weren't with the Feds. Then they gave us a couple of bottles and told us where they'd actually seen a Sasquatch. We didn't find anything that night and it took us two days to find our way out of the forest. We must not have followed their directions right."

Andy choked on another laugh. He'd bet those moonshiners had been hoping Joss and Mike would never make it out alive. Probably figured the moonshine and the forest would take care of them. Joss' uncanny luck had struck again, apparently.

Jenna lifted one hand to rub at her temples as her eyes closed and a long, deep sigh issued from her lips. When she spoke, she formed each word carefully, as if she might trip over them.

"Mike. Please help the man out of your trunk."

Mike's mouth fell open in shock. "But he might fly away."

Another sigh and her cute little teeth sank into her bottom lip before she took another deep breath. "Mike. If you don't get that guy out of your car, I'm going to call the cops and the only flying anyone will do is you through the legal system and straight into the loony bin!"

Looked like Jenna had reached her breaking point. Not that Andy could blame her. He'd get frustrated if he had to deal with this yahoo.

Mike blinked up at her, frozen like a deer in headlights. An angry Jenna definitely was a sight to behold. Her eyes blazed with heat, her cheeks flushed a pretty pink. When she put her hands on her hips, her breasts jutted out and nearly made his tongue fall out of his mouth.

Fry chose that moment to regain consciousness. He yawned, tried to stretch before he realized he didn't have enough room then sat up with a jaw-cracking yawn.

He had Jenna's and Mike's full attention as Fry threw his legs over the end of the car and rubbed at his eyes...with the ends of his wings.

Andy heard Jenna gasp. And Mike said, "See? I told you he was a fairy."

Then Mike turned to Andy, his head cocked to the side. Andy had seen that expression before.

It was the look true believers got when first confronted with proof that there were little green men. Only they didn't come from Mars. More like Ireland.

Crossing his arms over his chest, Andy just stared back.

Then, since he couldn't resist, he flipped the switch. For five seconds, with Jenna's attention solely on Fry and Andy completely out of her sightlines, he shifted into his Yeti form.

His body grew taller and broader, his form closer to a bear. His shaggy white fur gleamed in the sunlight and Andy bared a mouthful of sharp teeth in a shit-eating grin.

Five seconds was usually all it took for the yokels to realize what had happened. Unless they were dumber than the average yokel.

Apparently Mike was average. His mouth dropped open as his eyes widened. He literally froze, like a kid playing statue. Andy wanted to laugh but knew he'd give himself away with his growl.

Then Andy flipped the switch again and Mike gave a high-pitched squeal worthy of a tween girl who'd just found out her parents still had sex.

Jenna didn't appear to hear him or, if she had, she totally ignored him.

Moving to her side, Andy knew it was time for the reckoning. Because Jenna was not your average yokel. She might be the smartest person he'd ever met. Her brain never stopped working.

Except for right now when she looked like Eymorgs had stolen her brain, just waiting for someone to press a button and turn her on again.

"Hey, Andy." Fry grinned up at him from the car, his eyes bleary and his grin lopsided. "What the hell happened to you last night, buddy? You disappeared and I had to take care of those tengu all by myself."

Jenna blinked again then looked between him and Fry. Between that blink and the next, Jenna's brain began to compute.

And what she came up with equaled a hell of a lot more than four.

"Why does this man have wings?"

"Jenna…"

Mike tried to break into the conversation at that point but Jenna held up one hand and Mike closed up like a clam when she turned her sharp gaze on him.

"How did you know to look for me in Andy's cottage? Joss called this morning to tell me to go home. After he practically begged me to come up here and check out…this town."

Andy caught her slight hesitation and knew exactly what she'd been going to say. Joss had somehow found out about the Mystyk and sent Jenna to investigate. She'd been blissfully unaware of what she'd been about to stumble onto and now she was going to be either pissed off or scarred for life.

There was no way out of this situation without a little heartache for either of them. He just hoped Jenna didn't freak. He hated when women he really liked freaked out because they'd slept with him.

He'd been hoping he could see her again.

Damn it, he really didn't want this to be the end of their relationship. He *liked* Jenna. They had a connection that went beyond a geek's love of *Star Trek*.

But first he had to deal with Mike, because ole Mikey was hiding something.

And he wasn't doing a very good job of it if the flush covering his face was anything to go by.

"Joss was worried about me. Why was that, Mike?"

Seems Jenna had come to the same conclusion Andy had. That the only trouble Jenna was in was from Mike.

Which proved to be only too true when Mike pulled a gun. The hand holding the gun shook so much, Andy didn't think the guy would be able to hit the broad side of a barn. But at this close distance, he wouldn't even have to aim. A wild shot could hit any of them.

"Joss was worried I'd find the truth about the Mystyk before you did. And he was right. Now I'm going to be the one who gets the TV and book deals. I'm going to be famous. Everyone will talk about me when I show them a real, live fairy."

"I do prefer fae," Fry pointed out from the back of the Gremlin, where he continued to sit. "Fairy has such a distasteful connotation these days. Of course—"

"Fry." Andy kept his voice in a pleasant, *everything's just fine* tone. "Could we discuss this after the nice man has put the gun away?"

Fry hiccupped then covered his mouth with his hand to cover a burp. "Of course. But why does the nice man have a gun? That doesn't seem very nice to me."

Mike waved the gun in Andy's direction as if he was going to twirl it baton-style. "I have a gun because I'll shoot you with it if you don't do what I say."

Andy would do anything as long as the guy didn't point the gun in Jenna's direction again. He held up his hands in classic "Dude, don't shoot me" position.

But Jenna… Jenna wasn't taking any shit.

Before he realized what she was about to do, Jenna pulled back her arm and cold-cocked Mike.

In a scene worthy of an 80s *Power Rangers* episode, the gun flew out of Mike's hand and landed in Fry's lap, who brushed it onto the ground and under the car. Mike went down in a heap.

And Jenna began to curse like a sailor as she shook out her hand before she turned to him.

"I want to know what's going on right now." Without glancing away from Andy, she put her hand out toward Mike, who'd made a slight motion toward getting up. "You move and I will make sure you sing soprano for life."

Andy sighed. "You know all those things you're brother believes in? They're true."

Then he flicked the switch again.

Jenna didn't think her mouth could open any wider than it was right now.

I so owe Joss an apology.

It was the only thing she could think as the creature that had once been Andy raised a shaggy paw and waved at her.

Like Chewbacca. Damn, he looked like a freaking Wookie.

A white wookie, actually. And strangely…cute. Shaggy white fur that didn't look straggly at all. Actually it looked as if it'd been recently brushed. Like a show dog before judging.

Behind her, she heard something fall to the ground. And the fairy—sorry, the fae, began to laugh. "Well, that's one way to shut the guy up."

"I…I…"

Her brain kept trying to tell her that that…creature…was Andy.

Andy was the Abominable Snowman. No, wait…what did Joss call them? Yetis.

Yeah. Sure. Andy was a Yeti. Made perfect sense.

Bumbles bounce.

She blinked as the world began to darken, despite the fact that the sun was shining overhead. Passing out became a distinct possibility.

"Uh, Andy? She's looking a little…pasty."

She turned to look at the guy with the wings and couldn't help but grin when he waved at her with the tip of one of those beautiful, blue-tinted appendages.

Holy crap. The guy had blue wings.

And the man she'd slept with last night was a Yeti.

She had to tell Joss. She had to apologize for not believing in him. For occasionally thinking he was a crackpot and secretly patting herself on the back for being the sane sibling.

Joss was going to be a millionaire. A superstar. Forget about a cable show, he was going to make movies and…and…

She blinked and Andy stood in front of her again as a man. The hunky man he'd been before he'd turned into a seven-foot, white-haired snow monster.

Or—

No. She was going crazy. That's all there was too it.

"Jenna, I think you need to breathe," Andy said.

She automatically sucked in a deep breath and realized she'd been about to hyperventilate.

"What are you?"

She had to hear him say it. Had to know she wasn't going crazy and seeing things that weren't really there.

Andy's chin went up and he drew himself to his full height, an impressive sight.

Then he bowed and Jenna had the urge to curtsy.

"I'm a member of the Yeti tribe. My home is in Nepal but most of the younger tribe members no longer live in the village of our ancestors." His voice had taken on the cadence of the guy who narrated a lot of the whacked-out shows on the History Channel, odd breaks and all. "Now we travel the world, spreading—"

Fry reached out and smacked his arm.

"Please excuse him." Fry's words still slurred a bit and, combined with the accent, she was charmed. "He tends to get a little ferklempt," *hic,* "when he talks about his roots."

Andy shrugged. "Well, it's kind of cold in Nepal and we get kind of sick of snow and all the freakin' tourists. Yeah, we've got fur coats when we want them, but it's still getting crowded in our neck of the woods."

"And you're really a…a Bigfoot?"

"No, my cousin's a Sasquatch. I'm a Yeti."

"Of course he is."

"Jenna, you know I would never hurt you, right?"

She rolled her eyes at him. The thought hadn't even had time to cross her mind, and now… Well, of course he wouldn't hurt her. The guy who'd rocked her boat last night wouldn't hurt her. And neither would the hulking, seven-foot white wookie. "Did you ever meet George Lucas?"

As Fry nearly fell out of the back of the car laughing, Andy's adorable face screwed up in a frown. "Uh, no, I don't think— Oh, wait. You think I'm a freakin' wookie?"

Uh-oh. Jenna bit into her bottom lip at his offended tone. "I'm sorry. I actually think they're cute."

Fry did fall out of the car then, blue wings wrapped around his shoulders as he howled with laughter.

"Jenna," Andy started then stopped to shake his head. "I'm sorry too. I'm sorry you got dragged into this."

Damn, she totally knew where this was going. When a guy started telling you he was sorry for something, either he was about to tell you he'd cheated on you or he was dumping you.

And since it couldn't be the first, all things considered, it had to be the second. Which totally sucked, even though she understood. Really, she did.

What had she been expecting anyway? A lifelong commitment? She'd gone into this with the idea that it would be a fling and that was what she'd gotten.

A fling with a guy who could turn into a Yeti. Which, up until this moment, she hadn't believed existed.

It was enough to make a rational girl believe she needed a straitjacket and a rubber room.

And Jenna was nothing if not rational. Maybe too rational.

Maybe she needed to be a little irrational sometimes. Maybe she actually wanted to continue the romance with the Yeti.

Yeah, and what should she tell her brother?

Guess what, Joss? I met this great guy and he fulfills all my fantasies. And he's an abominable snow monster and would prove all your crazy theories and make you famous. And make Andy's life unbearable.

She couldn't do it.

Better to leave now and promise to keep his secret. Besides, no one would believe her. They'd think she was just another crackpot. Just like Joss.

She forced a bright smile. "I'm not sorry to have met you, Andy. And I won't betray your secret, not even to my brother. But what are you going to do with Mike?"

"Mike won't be a problem. We've got ways of making him keep quiet. Jenna..."

Andy looked pained, so at odds with his normal expression that she lifted her hand to stroke away the lines.

"You don't have to worry about me. I won't tell a soul." Not only would no one but her brother believe her but she'd be lumped into the same category of flake as her brother...which wasn't so flaky anymore.

"I should be going. I've got a long drive home and I have to work tomorrow."

Back to her boring life of numbers and equations and boring people who thought wookies weren't as cute as ewoks.

And that sometimes the things that went bump in the night were actually more interesting than the people who sleepwalked through their day believing the only strange things in life were people who thought *K* was an acceptable substitute for *C* in given names.

How could she reconcile her boring life to the one he lived?

"Jenna," Andy sighed. "Are you sure you're okay to drive?"

"Yes, I'll be fine. Really, I will." Maybe not her heart but…

"I know this is a lot to take in. And I totally understand that you don't want to talk to me right now. But, if you find you do need someone to talk to later, look up Carrie Benson. She works as a reporter for the *Weekly World News* in West Reading. She's been in the same situation as you."

"Carrie Benson. Sure." Of course he wasn't offering to come visit her himself. She figured as soon as she was gone, he'd go jetting off to another part of the country. Or the world. He was a freakin' *Yeti*.

"Jenna."

Instead of answering the entreaty in his eyes, she turned and took a step back rather than throwing herself at him then turned and forced herself to start walking.

Back to normal life. Which, after today, was going to be completely overrated. And oh so lonely.

Chapter Seven

"Jenna, are you sure you're okay? You don't sound like yourself."

"I'm fine, Joss. Honestly. Nothing's wrong. Tell me how the shooting's going?"

For a few seconds, Jenna thought Joss wasn't going to let her change the subject. He'd called her every day for the past week. Every time his question seemed legitimate.

Hey, Jenna, can you stop by my apartment and make sure I locked the back door?

Hey, Jenna, do you think I need to see a doctor for this rash on my leg?

Hey, Jenna, will you check to see if I paid the bill for my cryogenic storage chamber?

But she knew he was checking up on her. And here she thought she'd been doing a good job of hiding her depression.

She missed Andy. Which was ridiculous. She'd only known him for a day. Sure, it'd been the best sex of her life but he was a globe-trotting Yeti shapeshifter.

She was an accountant who lived in a house with a spotless white kitchen. Whose white kitchen was ever spotless?

As Joss finally began to talk about the fact that he was shooting at Loch Ness and how cool that was and how he'd only fallen off the boat twice, once on purpose, Jenna let her mind drift.

Back to Andy, of course. She wondered what he'd think of her if he saw her now, slouched in her black chair in her bland, cream-colored office with mahogany furniture, everything neatly in its place. Her books arranged by subject and her file cabinets meticulously alphabetized.

Even the diplomas on her walls were perfectly level.

"God, I'm the most boring person on earth."

"What? Who told you that? I'll kick their a—"

"I'm sorry, Joss. I'm going to have to call you back. I've decided I'm sick of living in a world without wookies."

Silence for a full five seconds. "Uh, Jenna, are you sure you feel okay?"

"Cookies. I mean cookies. I'm on one of those stupid diets again."

"You don't need a diet, Jenna. Did someone tell you need to be on a diet? They're full of shit. You're perfect just the way you are."

She actually felt tears come to her eyes at her brother's defense. "I love you, Joss."

"Yeah, love you too. And Jenna?"

"Yeah?"

"Nobody wants to live in a world without wookies."

* * * * *

"Well, it's not every day my accountant comes to visit. I hope you're not bearing bad news."

Jenna kept her smile as bright as she could even though she wanted to wince at the volume of Bill Dailey's voice.

The short, round and balding editor of the *Weekly News Journal* always spoke as if he had to be heard over a jet engine.

"No bad news, Bill." She took his outstretched hand and let him shake until she thought her arm would fall off. "How are you doing?"

"Can't complain, can't complain. Well, I could, but nobody listens."

Jenna didn't know how anyone could fail to listen but, as she looked around the office filled with several messy desks and a few antiquated pieces of office equipment, she saw no one paid him the least amount of attention.

"Anyway, we're still making payroll, so that's good," Bill continued. "We've actually seen an increase in subscriptions lately so that's even better. Lot more tinfoil-hat-wearing people out there than you might think." He left off with a bray that reached ear-splitting levels before cutting off. "And since you've been working your magic on our books, we've managed to make a profit, as you well know."

Yes, the *Journal* had made a tiny bit of money last year. Enough to buy a couple of high-end computers for the graphic designers. Or, as Bill called them, the wizard geeks.

"So what can I do for you, Jenna?"

"Actually, I'd like to talk to Carrie Benson, if she's here. She and I are serving on a committee together and I just need a few minutes of her time."

The lie rolled right off her tongue, amazingly enough, without a telltale blush or stutter. She'd had to practice but she figured she'd be getting a lot more practice if this went well.

Bill barely paused. "Care! Get over here."

"Jesus freakin' crap, Bill, I'm right here."

Jenna did jump then because the voice came from right behind her. She turned to find herself staring at a rather well-endowed woman. A woman who could pass for an Amazon. She stood at least six feet tall, was perfectly proportioned and had long auburn hair that hung around a pretty face. And sharp green eyes that stared at her intently even though her smile was easy. And knowing.

"Hey, Jenna. Nice to see you again."

This woman lied even better than Jenna, who caught back a sigh of relief before Bill could notice. Carrie was going to play along. Did that mean Andy had told Carrie about her?

"Hi, Carrie. Sorry to bother you at work but do you think we could talk for a few minutes? I just have a few things—"

"See ya later, Jenna. Have a nice day. Things to do." Bill patted her on the back, which nearly made her topple over then headed for a guy slouched in a chair in the back corner. "Jamey, where the hell's that picture of the alien baby autopsy?"

Jamey gave Bill the finger.

"Why don't we go into the break room?" Carrie motioned toward the front of the office on the second floor of a quiet building in West Reading. "Should be quiet."

Jenna gave a short nod then followed along, her eye catching several times on the *Journal* covers plastered on the wall.

Aliens Ate My Baby!

Wolf Boy Spotted with Lizard Man in Philadelphia Sewer!

A Weekend in the Alps with My Yeti Boyfriend!

She paused at that one, her eye caught by the incredible likeness to Andy in his Yeti form. Almost as if someone had taken a picture of him then made it just blurry enough to look fake.

"Like that one? I think it's one of my best."

Carrie wore that grin again, the one that said she was in on the joke, whatever that joke might be. Right now, the joke appeared to be on Jenna.

"Did you take that?"

"Sure did, right over the Berks County line in the woodlands in Schuylkill County."

"It's an incredible shot."

"Thanks. Amazing what you can do with Photoshop these days, isn't it?"

Except Carrie and Jenna knew that photo hadn't been altered to insert a picture of the Yeti. The only alteration Carrie had done had been to make the photo look as fake as possible.

"So." Carrie waved her into the lunchroom and closed the door behind her. "What can I do for you? Since we both know we're not serving on a committee together."

Jenna jumped in with both feet since Carrie didn't look like the kind of person who put up with any bullshit. "I need to get in touch with Andy."

"Andy who?" Carrie crossed her arms over her chest and leaned against the nearest table. She still wore an easy expression but Jenna could tell the other woman was waiting for Jenna to say the right thing. Or the wrong thing.

"Andy Lohani. We met last weekend in Tioga County when my brother sent me to investigate a bar where he believed supernatural creatures hang out. Except they're not creatures. They're people. I met Andy, who…" She paused, not knowing how much she should say in a room that wasn't soundproofed or swept for bugs. "Well, when I freaked after we were nearly shot by my brother's friend, I told Andy goodbye."

Which she'd regretted since the moment she'd driven away. "Biggest mistake of my life. So I'm here to beg you to give Andy a message from me. I've kept my promise. I've told no one. I will never tell anyone his secrets. Or the secrets of his friends. I just want to see him again and apologize."

Carrie stared at her for a few seconds before shoving that gorgeous red hair over her shoulder and leaning down until her eyes and Jenna's were on the same level.

"I'm not saying I believe your crazy story, Jenna, because really, who believes in supernatural creatures?" Carrie's smile was back and this time it had a bit of a hard edge. "They're just figments of our imagination and fodder for crazy tabloid stories, right? Or a way for a guy to make a living traipsing around the world shooting documentaries with fuzzy film footage and fading footprints in snow."

Jenna tried to keep her disappointment from showing. Carrie wasn't going to help her. Andy must have told her that, if Jenna came looking for him, Carrie should pull a *Men in Black* and deny everything.

Jenna understood. She really did.

She was a clone living with other clones on the Death Star while Andy and his friends hung out on the much cooler Millennium Falcon.

"But," Carrie continued, "just for the sake of argument, let's say these people really did exist. Don't you think they'd be understandably gun-shy about getting close to anyone who wasn't born in their world? How the slightest hint of rejection might make them more than a little reluctant to let anyone have a second chance. Sometimes you have to be willing to put yourself out there a little further."

Hope began to bubble. "Sounds like you have a little experience with that."

Carrie shrugged. "A little."

"And how would you suggest I do this?"

"Are you sure you're really ready to embrace the crazy? Because I gotta tell you, there are days when you're gonna wonder if you're ever going to see the other side of the rabbit hole again."

Jenna nodded. She'd been living on the other side for way too long. She wanted Andy and she was willing to step into a little weird. "I'm positive. I haven't thought of anyone or anything since I left Andy. I'm willing to do what it takes to show him I'm not going anywhere."

Now Carrie's smile was genuine. "Then consider yourself invited to a little party."

* * * * *

Jenna almost turned around at the end of the lane leading to Carrie's boyfriend's house.

She'd actually been hoping the GPS would talk her out of this crazy idea but the stubborn thing had remained silent the entire way.

Hell, the damn thing hadn't even acknowledged that there was a house out here, much less a road that led to it.

Carrie had warned her to carefully follow her written directions because otherwise, she'd never find it. Carrie had been right.

Jenna had missed the last turn and had had to execute a three-point turn worthy of a stunt driver.

"What if he doesn't want me here? What if he's already seeing someone else? What if he doesn't even remember me?"

Once again, the GPS totally ignored her.

Jenna frowned. "Bitch. Just wait until the next time you tell me to take a left. I'm definitely going right."

Since she'd finally gone off her rocker, she figured she might as well park at the end of the line of cars along the lane and make her way to the house.

From here, she could see the beautiful log home—and the crowd of people hanging out in the yard.

Getting out of the car, she smoothed her costume down, wondering if anyone would realize she was dressed as Princess Leia visiting the Ewok Village in *The Empire Strikes Back*. She'd made the tan-and-white dress by hand when she'd briefly dated a *Star Wars* fanatic and it hadn't seen the light of day in years. Surprisingly it still fit. But back then, her hair had been long enough to mimic Carrie Fisher's and she hadn't felt as awkward as she did now.

When that romance had fizzled, Jenna had packed away her dress and stuck it in a closet behind her *Star Trek*, *Next Gen* and *Enterprise* uniforms.

"Maybe you have way too much time on your hands and need to get a life."

Then again, she might just fit in here more than she'd imagined.

The party had spilled out of the house and there were at least twenty people hanging out in the yard.

All of them wore elaborate costumes. It looked like a backwoods version of Comic-Con, complete with two Dr. Whos, a Captain Jack Harkness and someone who looked like Gary Oldman's Dracula monster.

As she drew closer, she realized that last one *wasn't* a costume. Oh-kay.

Captain Kirk and Spock had their arms around each other, bringing to mind a fan illustration she'd seen as a teenager. Back then she'd been stunned at the insinuation that her childhood heroes had a thing for each other. As an adult, well…she got it. And read the fanfic.

Now though, she could only wonder if Spock's oversized, pointed ears were real. Guess she was about to find out.

As she walked toward the house, she didn't see Andy but Carrie had assured her he'd be there. Andy loved a good party.

And if she wasn't mistaken she did see Fry, blue wings on display as he chatted to a couple of women dressed as Buffy and Faith, vampire slayers.

Except they had hooves.

Deep breath. Don't stare. And for god's sake, don't pet anyone.

Except maybe the blue tiger lounging on the grass in a patch of sun.

Captain Jack noticed her first. He approached with a wide grin on his handsome face and an outstretched hand. He looked nothing like John Barrowman though he did look completely human. And only four feet tall.

"Hello, my dear, and welcome. It's nice to see a new face at one of our shindigs. My name's—"

"Gonna be Mud if you don't take your little hands off her, Darwin." Fry strolled over and grabbed Jenna's hand before she could take the other man's. "The woman's spoken for. Hello again, pretty Jenna. I'm glad you showed up."

It was hard not to smile at Fry. He really was almost blindingly handsome and his eyes blazed like sapphires. "Hello, Fry. It's nice to see you. Is…is Andy here?"

"If you can call sulking in a corner 'here', well then, yes, he is. Why don't you let me show you where to find him?"

Leaving a sulking Darwin behind them, they made their way

through the crowd, many of whom stopped to stare at her. They knew she wasn't like them, probably wondered why she was here at all.

A few of the women gave her dirty looks. One might have even hissed at her but Fry glared and she backed off. But not after giving Jenna a fanged grin. Seriously, the woman had fangs. Real ones.

Inside, bodies filled the open living space. Almost all of them stood over six feet tall.

She saw Carrie first, standing next to a handsome guy who had to be almost as tall as Andy but he had the most amazingly gorgeous brunet hair, all shades of browns and golds and reds. Damn, the guy was gorgeous. Not as beautiful as Andy but still...

As Fry continued to pull her farther into the room, she tried to spot her Yeti but there were several other guys there with blond hair. A few of them had to be related to Andy, the resemblance was so close.

But still not the man she wanted.

Fry kept moving through the crowd, not stopping to talk to the few people who called out to him. He appeared to have a specific destination and a single-minded determination to get there.

They'd crossed the entire width of the house before she finally saw him.

Her own Han Solo, dressed in leather pants and vest with a white shirt and a blaster on his hip.

What more proof did she need that they were meant for each other?

Andy stood at a window at the back of the house, staring out into the trees. The sun glinted off his hair, pulling out gold highlights. The man truly was stunning.

And even though she didn't have claws, she was going to scratch the eyes out of the girl standing next to him, doing everything in her power to fall out of her skimpy Princess Leia slave costume. She had long, dark hair and a pretty face but Andy didn't seem to notice the hussy.

And when Fry called out, "Hey, Andy, I got a present for you," he didn't even turn from the window.

"I'm not doing another of those redheaded sluts, Fry. The last ones tasted like cough syrup."

"I don't think you're going to object to this present. Not when she seems perfect for you."

Andy turned then, his eyes lighting up when he caught sight of her. "Jenna!"

The unfeigned pleasure in his voice made her smile and when Andy took a step toward her, she threw caution to the wind and threw herself at him. She trusted he'd catch her and she wasn't disappointed.

She ended up with her arms around his neck, her feet a foot off the floor and her mouth sealed against his.

Nowhere else she'd rather be.

* * * * *

By the time they reached Jenna's house, they'd circled back around to the starting point of their conversation.

"I know it's going to take some work but I'm not ready to give you up yet, Jenna. I shouldn't have let you walk away that day."

"And I'm sorry for walking away. I was worried that I wouldn't fit into your life. I mean, I don't even know what you do for a living or where you live."

"Most of my family is in the travel business. We facilitate tourists coming into Nepal. I act as liaison to the travel companies all over the world, though mostly in the US."

"Where do you live?"

"Nowhere, really. I mean, I've got an apartment in Nepal and one in New York City and Frisco but that doesn't mean I can't work out of somewhere smaller, like, say, Reading?"

"But what about my brother? He's going to take one look at you and know."

Andy hadn't gotten around to telling Jenna that he'd heard an interesting story about Joss in the past couple of days. A story that, if it were true, might just change the way Joss looked at the world.

"We'll worry about that when it happens. I've gotten pretty good at hiding in plain sight."

Jenna looked as if she was about to say something else but they'd finally reached her neighborhood. Finally, Andy pulled his truck to a stop at the curb.

Jenna's neighborhood should've been in the dictionary next to the definition of suburban.

All small brick homes probably built in the 50s. Square little boxes that had been modified over the years until they each had their own personality.

Jenna's looked like a dollhouse. Her exterior had been painted white, the shutters were a deep purple, the front door bright yellow. The expansive flower beds mimicked those same colors. Only a couple of patches of grass remained in the front yard and the front porch was a square of white concrete filled with pots of plants.

It looked so…normal.

Until he noticed the gnome peeking out of one of the beds. And the fairy and the gargoyles. And the… "Where did you find garden statues of the Argonath?"

She smiled as she slid out of his SUV then waited for him to join her on the sidewalk before heading toward the front door. Actually, they almost ran. If any of her neighbors were watching, they probably had a good laugh as Andy nearly tripped over his own feet watching Jenna hurry to the front door and throw it open.

"Do you really want to talk about my *Lord of the Rings* obsession right now or would you rather be naked in bed?"

Good thing he'd already made it up the steps or he'd probably be on his face.

As it was, he barely remembered to duck as he stepped through the door, which flew shut behind him as Jenna shoved it then began tearing at his clothes.

"How about naked on the couch. It's closer."

"Fine by me."

"Wait. Can you leave the dress on?"

"Only if you leave the pants."

"For you, baby, anything."

She pulled back to smile at him, the way he was already addicted to, then lifted her skirt. She was bare beneath it.

His heart nearly stopped before beginning to thump like a heavy metal drum line. "Holy crap, Jenna. If I'd known you were naked under there, we'd be doing it in the car on Tim's lane."

"I think I like my couch better."

"I think you should come here now."

Instead of obeying his not very forceful command, she reached for his pants.

He groaned. "Okay, that works too."

She didn't tease him. No, his Jenna was practical about it. She wanted his pants open, she opened his pants. And when she had them down low enough that she could get her hands around his cock, she began stroking him even as she maneuvered him until he sank onto the couch.

He was pretty sure he heard something creak beneath him but then Jenna lifted her skirt again and placed one knee on either side of his hips.

He got a peek at her pretty pussy, and he was gone. Normal had never felt so good.

Leaning forward, she feathered her mouth against his as she brushed the lips of her sex against the tip of his cock.

He groaned, the sound rumbling against his ribs, and felt Jenna's mouth curve in a smile.

When he grabbed her hips, ready to pull her down onto him, she put her hands over his and shook her head. "No, no. This time, we're playing by my rules."

"Honey, as long as your rules say you're not going anywhere anytime soon, I'm good with that."

She released him and cupped his face in her hands, staring into his eyes with a smile. "Now why would I want to go anywhere when here is pretty damn good?"

Her hips moved again, eliciting another groan from him as she rubbed against his length. Her juices coated his cock in slick heat as her lips closed over his.

He opened his mouth when her tongue flicked against his lips, which parted to allow her access. Her tongue slid into his mouth and played with his, tormenting him, until he couldn't take it anymore and took over the kiss.

He sank his hands into her hair and pulled her even closer, her breasts pressing against his chest.

Sliding one hand from her hair, he trailed his fingers along her neck until he reached the neckline of her dress.

Stretchy. Good.

He pulled it down until he freed one breast. "No bra," he said against her lips. "I admire your authenticity."

"More like I didn't have a bra that wouldn't show."

"All the better for me."

Wrapping one arm around her waist, he lifted her until he had the right angle for his lips to suck on one puckered nipple.

Her breathless sigh made his blood pound and he licked and sucked until her hips ground against his abdomen and his cock was so hard, he could probably hit home runs with it.

"Andy."

He really loved the way she said his name when he had his teeth on her nipple.

"Yeah?"

"I want you. Right now."

But he hadn't tasted her other breast yet. So he ignored her until he'd sufficiently played with that one as well.

By the time he leaned back, Jenna had a death grip on his hair and a beatific look on her face.

Not that he was unaffected. Hell, his muscles shook with the strain of holding steady, of not yanking her down onto his cock and forcing her to ride him like a cowgirl.

Now, though... It was definitely time.

"Jenna."

Her eyes opened to a half slit, dark and mysterious. "Yes."

That definitely wasn't a question.

With a slight adjustment, she repositioned herself, her sex closing around the head of his cock.

As she sank onto him in slow, measured strokes, he watched her eyes close as bliss transformed her expression.

Heat shot through him. From his cock to his balls to his spine, where it spread out like lightning. She rode him just like he'd imagined she would, just hard enough to rattle him but slow enough to make him want to beg. Sinking her teeth into his earlobe, she tugged then licked the tiny hurt. "I think I'm gonna like living on the Fringe, Andy."

Grabbing her hips, he couldn't wait any longer. He began to thrust hard and fast.

His balls tightened, his cock throbbed and he lost the battle. With his arms tight around her, he gasped out her name as he came. Just before she did the same.

"If this is normal, babe," he said, still trying to catch his breath, "it's way more fun than I ever gave it credit for."

The End

STEPHANIE JULIAN

Stephanie Julian has been a daily news reporter, a freelance feature writer and a movie, theater and music critic but what she loves most is writing heat with heart. She's happily married to a Springsteen fanatic and is the mother of two sons.

THANK YOU FOR READING!

If you enjoyed this book, please consider leaving a review. It will help others find this story.